Goods & Effects

Testimonials

One of the most interesting reads I've experienced in a long time. Description of rural life is amazing, ... episodic style so cinematic. And I found myself invested in Hannah from the very beginning. I loved the characters who populate her world.—**Andrew Campbell, Arts Manager for the City of West Hollywood (Retired)**

*****

The characters and environment are really well drawn, the settings and scenes are interesting, and the image of Hannah driving country roads, encountering people and touching (and being touched by) their lives is such a lovely idea.—**Michael Hofacre, Filmmaker, Los Angeles**

*****

What a great read! There were so many satisfying twists and complex characters. Hannah is such a strong protagonist. I hated to put the book down.—**Glynis Whiting, Novelist and Film Director**

Goods & Effects

by

Al Schnupp

Golden Antelope Press
715 E. McPherson
Kirksville, Missouri 63501
2021

ISBN: 978-1-952232-55-8

Library of Congress Control Number: 2021931896

Published by:
Golden Antelope Press
715 E. McPherson
Kirksville, Missouri 63501

Available at:
Golden Antelope Press
715 E. McPherson
Kirksville, Missouri, 63501
Phone: (660) 665-0273
http://www.goldenantelope.com
Email: ndelmoni@gmail.com

Acknowledgements

Goods & Effects was conceived as a screenplay. For years it hibernated in my file cabinet. After retiring as a professor of theatre, I resurrected the decades-old story and decided to transpose it into a piece of prose. Recrafting the story became a process of revisiting my past, re-examining my heritage, reimagining *"what if?"* I am grateful to Wyatt Brown, a supportive and generous friend, the first to read each draft and offer his reaction. Thank you to Andrew Campbell, Michael Hofacre and Glynis Whiting for their encouragement. I am indebted to Erma Stauffer; given our similar backgrounds, sharing the stories of our journeys has been comforting, cathartic, humorous and inspirational. I am beholden to Gene Hayworth whose feedback prompted me to fill in missing gaps. Many thanks to Betsy Delmonico, an invaluable guide, giving excellent editorial advice, suggesting avenues for expanding the story.

Goods & Effects

Hannah was told by Deacon Stahl her husband would not be given a church funeral.

"The cemetery is reserved for those confirmed in the faith," Mr. Stahl reminded Hannah, eyeing the tray of cinnamon rolls on the counter.

Hannah opened a drawer and withdrew a sharp knife.

All her life she had attended Creekside Mennonite Church.

Slowly she cut into the soft, glazed buns, separating a corner pillow from its neighbors.

Just before her eleventh birthday, Hannah had confessed her sins, accepted Jesus as her savior and was welcomed into the fold.

She opened an overhead cupboard and selected a small plate. Bone china, rimmed with a wreath of ivy leaves and delicate violets. A gift from her grandmother.

Hannah's conversion had been followed by several weeks of carefully orchestrated instruction in the ways of the church. On a cloudless spring morning, the sunlight blanching the plain white walls of the sanctuary, she was baptized along with two other girls and a stout lad, looking like he preferred pledging himself to the devil.

"My eye tells me those rolls were made by Eddie," Mr. Stahl said, licking the corners of his mouth.

1

"Indeed. They were." The bakery, in just a few short months, had shamed its competitors.

"Eddie's quite accomplished," sniffed Stahl, "at doing a woman's work."

Hannah lifted the bun, placed it on the plate and handed it to Deacon Stahl, along with a fork.

"And my sons?"

Ignoring the utensil, the deacon lifted the roll and bit down. He registered his satisfaction before speaking.

"Your sons ...." He paused, as if to say, "Might I have a glass of milk?"

Hannah crossed her arms.

"They are innocent. Too young to recognize their standing in the eyes of God. We will permit them to be interred in the cemetery."

Hannah bit her lower lip. She nodded. "Thank you."

There are certain smells that capture and celebrate life on the farm, Hannah thought. Fresh mown hay, its aroma as lifting as a hymn. The smell of seasoned corn, chopped into fodder, with its traces of vinegar and heady, ground reeds. Although Stahl was no farmer or tenderer of livestock, Hannah thought he smelled like neglected sheep.

The deacon surveyed the counter, brimming with apricot cobbler, rhubarb pie, angel food cake, Toll House cookies, mint brownies. He imagined, correctly, the refrigerator was stocked with casseroles, plastic containers of potato salad, plates of sliced ham, herbed stuffing and jars of gravy. From a side pocket, he pulled out and unrolled a map of Creekside Cemetery.

"The areas in red are unclaimed. Perhaps you would like to pick out a plot for Gerald and Simon. I'll have the groundskeeper prepare the site."

Hannah shook her head. "I want my sons buried by their father."

"Oh?" Stahl shifted in his seat. "If it's a matter of cost, I'm sure I can find someone to purchase them for you."

"Thank you, Mr. Stahl. I've made up my mind."

"If I could ask, where will you inter your family?"

Hannah walked to the open rollup desk and pulled an envelope from one of its compartments.

"I've spoken to the Director of Zoning at the Kalb County Courthouse. I was granted permission to bury my family on the farm."

Stahl was puzzled. "I would think a child of God would want his kin buried in a proper graveyard. One sanctified by the church."

"Would you like the plate of brownies to take with you?"

"Well," Stahl stammered, "would you like me, or Pastor Lentz, to say a few words at the services?"

"What were you thinking?"

"Certainly, scripture seems in order. Something edifying. Perhaps a passage from Psalms."

"I'll let you know," Hannah concluded.

"Wonderful. I'll be happy to assist."

"But I would like to select the passage," interjected Hannah.

The deacon raised his eyebrows. Resisting the urge to confront Hannah, he simply said, "Brownies would be lovely."

"Give my regards to Naomi," she said, her eyes clouding over. "She knows I love her homemade banana ice cream."

The Mercer farm, nestled in the rolling hills of northeastern Missouri, had belonged to her husband's family for nearly sixty years. The farmhouse, barn and surrounding outbuildings were tucked on the side of a hill, above a meadow that bordered a small stream. Cultivated fields spread out along the south-facing property.

Often, when Hannah drove from the main road down the lane to the farm, observing the landscape, she understood why the practice of quilt-making was so popular in the region.

On the crest of the hill, above the farm, a solitary tree fingered the sky. Simon called the tree *Periscope*.

"Periscope? Isn't that an instrument to observe other ships at sea?" asked Hannah.

"The tree is observing the sky," Simon had replied.

After Deacon Stahl departed, Hannah pulled on a pair of boots. She walked out the lane, turned left and walked uphill. For a long while, she stood under the wide branches of *Periscope*, deep in thought. She continued onward, down the north side of the hill to her nearest neighbor, Frank and Norma Paulson. She found Frank, replacing the carburetor on his rusted, arthritic tractor.

He tipped his cap. "Hannah." He wasn't sure how to proceed.

Hannah waved her hand. "It's alright. There's nothing to be said."

"I'm sorry. Horace was a mighty fine man."

Before he could continue, Hannah interrupted. "I have a favor to ask you."

"Sure. Whatever you need."

"But in exchange, I want you to pick out a cow for yourself. No arguments."

"What's the favor?"

"Would you dig the graves for Horace and my sons? On the hilltop. Under the sycamore."

"I suppose I could borrow a backhoe from Jesse ...."

"Whatever it costs, I'll pay."

With the heel of his shoe, Frank made a small depression in the dirt.

"The church won't have anything to do with Horace," she said.

"It would be my honor," Frank conceded.

"I can't think of a better resting place," added Hannah.

Frank inclined his head and gazed into the distance.

Hannah registered his concern. "It's taken care of. You won't be breaking the law. How's Norma?"

"It's one of her better days, I think." Instantly he regretted his choice of words. "She's fine. A new medicine."

"I plan to hold the service on Sunday," Hannah explained. "Do you want me to ...?"

"Yes, if you could cover their graves after the service, that would be appreciated."

Frank removed his cap and wiped his brow. He nodded several times.

"You've been a wonderful neighbor," Hannah added. She reached out and touched Frank on the forearm.

"You're not leaving, are you? You're not getting rid of the farm?"

"I'm not saying anything at all. You've been a wonderful neighbor. That's all." She turned. As she walked away, passing the house, she thought she saw Norma looking out through the tired, yellow kitchen curtains.

Theo and Olle Jansson were strapping, nineteen-year-old twins, of Swedish stock. Whenever Horace needed to hire an extra hand, he enlisted the pair. They were blessed with rugged good looks, square jaws and a mop of unruly, playful blond hair. It was impossible to distinguish between the two until they smiled. Theo had a set of perfectly-cast teeth; Olle was gifted with a mouthful of ill-shaped, ill-formed teeth. Rather than distract from Olle's charm, his curse enhanced it. Along with Horace, the trio had replaced the roof on the equipment shed, built a small dam across the stream, and raced to harvest acres of alfalfa before oncoming storms.

At Hannah's request, the twins arrived at the farm at eight-thirty on Sunday morning. Olle had borrowed their uncle's open pickup truck and they sped up the driveway, the radio blaring, the deep-ribbed tires kicking up dust.

Theo turned down the radio and reminded Olle this was no time to be jovial. They were on a somber errand. Olle spun the truck around and backed it up to the front porch. The pair jumped out. Hannah greeted them just outside the front door.

"Would you like a glass of juice?" she asked.

"Sure!"

"No thanks."

"I'm more inclined to believe Olle,"Hannah said.

She led them to the living room where she pointed out the piano.

The pair lifted the upright Schimmel as though it were an empty cardboard box. They carried it through the kitchen, out the front door and placed it gently onto the bed of the pickup.

Hannah was there with two glasses of cold pear nectar.

"I had no idea you play piano, Mrs. Mercer," Olle said.

"Oh, I don't. This belonged to Horace."

The brothers exchanged unknowing looks.

"Horace was quite accomplished." She let her hands rest on the keys. "Ellie will be playing." She returned to the living room to retrieve the stool, which she handed to Theo.

"There's no need to unload the monster. Just leave it on the bed of the truck."

"Ellie Corvello?"

Theo elbowed Olle.

"Yes, boys, *the* gorgeous Italian Catholic Ellie. Give a Mennonite a piano and you get three chords. Played loudly. Horace had his standards. Which I aim to honor."

Theo climbed aboard the truck to hold the piano, and Olle took his place behind the driver's seat. Slowly, they made their way down the driveway and up the hill to *Periscope*.

If folks at Creekside Mennonite Church had issues with Hannah's choices - which indeed they did - they put them aside for the day. Members of the congregation showed up to offer their support and condolences. There would be time, tomorrow, and the days that followed, to chatter.

How does a wife, a devout Christian, prepare a funeral for a husband who professes no faith? Horace reserved his reverence for the sight of delicate, growing crops, a cow's affection for her calf, the beauty of a Bach sonata.

To open the ceremony, Hannah requested that Ellie play *Raindrop* by Fédéric Chopin. It was a piece Horace hoped to master, attempting with each study at the keyboard to find its subtle shifts in atmosphere. The rendition was not perfect. Ellie stumbled each time she turned a page, but she quickly regained her composure and slipped back into the song's gentle rhythm. The crowd listened intently, introduced to a friend they hadn't previously recognized.

Deacon Stahl, looking apologetic but with a tone of defiance, recited *The Lord's Prayer*.

"Simon's favorite book was *Charlotte's Web*," explained Hannah. "On many occasions, Simon asked Gerald to read the story to him. Not because Simon couldn't read, but because he loved being near his brother and hearing his voice." She paused, slowly opened the book, swept her hand across the page, and read:

> *These autumn days will shorten and grow cold. The leaves will shake loose from the trees and fall. Christmas will come, then the snows of winter. You will live to enjoy the beauty of the frozen world, for you mean a great deal to Zuckerman and he will not harm you, ever. Winter will pass, the days will lengthen, the ice will melt in the pasture pond. The song sparrow will return and sing, the frogs will awake, the warm wind will blow again. All these sights and sounds and smells will be yours to enjoy, Wilbur – this lovely world, these precious days....*

Hymnals were distributed. Ellie waited patiently on the bed of the truck, seated on the stool, her hands resting on her lap. Hannah nodded and Ellie began to play *What a Friend We Have in Jesus*, which the assembled mourners sang enthusiastically.

Have we trials and temptations?
Is there trouble everywhere?
We should never be discouraged;
Take it to the Lord in prayer.

Hannah seemed to hear the lyrics for the first time, from a new perspective. *We should never be discouraged.* Until now, she hadn't doubted their honesty. The words arose from roots that reached to her childhood. They were as true and dependable as stuffed dolls, birthday cakes and the yellow bus that ferried her to school. Until now.

That evening a neighbor, Harlen, came to help with the milking. Hannah joined him, patting the rumps of the cows so as not to startle them, washing down teats and slipping suction cups over their udders. Harlen distributed feed along the length of the trough, then walked the center aisle, scooping up droppings. Neither spoke a word.

Back in the kitchen, Hannah opened the refrigerator and studied its options. Nothing appealed to her.

The air was still and warm. She grabbed a shawl, threw it over her shoulders and began climbing the hill. Halfway to her destination, she dropped to her knees. Perhaps now it would be possible to cry.

She returned to the farmhouse and gazed at its unrecognizable silhouette, unable to express her grief. A solitary light burned in the kitchen.

Hannah walked up the barn's embankment, an earth-packed ramp leading to the second floor of the wood-bone structure. She threw open the doors and stepped inside. Before her was a green and yellow 1955 International Harvester Metro van. It once belonged to Horace's uncle, who used to deliver baked goods to grocery stores in several counties. The glass pane in the driver's door had been replaced with a roll-down window. When Horace acquired the vehicle, he removed the storage racks and used the truck to haul bags of seed corn, fertilizer and other farm supplies.

Hannah pushed aside the sliding door and slipped into the seat, unable to recall the last time she drove it. The keys were still in the ignition and the engine roared to life on the first try. Hannah released the brake lever, nudged her foot against the gas pedal and eased the van out the barn. She parked halfway between the barn and farmhouse where she had an unobstructed view of the makeshift graveyard.

She stared numbly out the window, at an incomprehensible truth. Five Paws jumped on the shallow hood of the truck, causing a startled Hannah to jump and knock her knee against the gear shift. She opened the door, gathered Five Paws in her arms and returned to the cab, where she leaned against the door. She wrapped the shawl around Five Paws and herself and waited for sleep.

In the morning, Hannah was awakened by the sound of crows that routinely held a stakeout on the milk house. Five Paws was seated on the dash, staring at her.

She turned her head and gazed at the front door to their home. It was no longer familiar. It seemed to be sealed shut by a sheet of plywood, its edges nailed tight. She looked in the side mirror. The two large doors to the second story of the barn remained open.

If she were to drive anywhere, she should have her license. But the card was in her purse in the house. She decided against getting it. It didn't seem to matter if she were caught breaking the law. Five Paws continued his steady, unbroken study of Hannah.

Absent a license and unsure if the vehicle registration was current, Hannah fired up the truck and rolled down the lane. After a few hiccups, the engine settled down.

She rolled down the window and drove to Martin's Feed Mill, just outside Adele. One could smell the scent of ground barley and oats before rounding the curve, crossing Calico Creek and catching sight of the mill behind a cluster of trees. Hannah immediately spotted Larry, seated on the loading dock next to the scales, mending burlap bags.

Larry Zimmerman stood and raised his cap, saluting the freakish truck with its bulldog snout, cat-nose grill and over-sized tires.

Hannah pulled up next to Larry. She rested her left elbow on the window ledge, tapping her fingernails lightly against the steering wheel.

"Morning, Mrs. Mercer."

"Larry, could you come out to the farm after work?"

"Sure." He cocked his head and looked skyward. "Your spark plugs could use a cleaning. What's up?"

"I have a job that needs muscle. The pay's good."

"You want me to bring my toolbox?"

"That would be useful. And bring Jake."

When Hannah returned home, Frank was milking the cows.

It touched Hannah how, without consulting her, Loretta showed up the day after the accident. At Creekside Mennonite, Loretta had assumed the role of battlefield nurse. Her favorite job was overseeing the creation of scrapbooks for the infirm. Rolling up the walkway in her wheelchair, Loretta stopped at the porch edge and handed Hannah a note.

"This is a list of the men who'll be helping with the milking." Written on the back of a calendar were the names of those who had volunteered their services. Twice a day, Sunday through Saturday, someone was scheduled to perform the chore. Every farmer at Creekside Mennonite was on the schedule. But the list included a number of Lutherans, Methodists and freethinkers, too, who, without prompting, assumed it was their duty to volunteer.

Five Paws led the way to the milk house where Hannah scooped up a dipperful of milk from the cooling tank and poured in into a tin can.

"How much is a cow worth these days?" Hannah asked Frank.

"I'd estimate two hundred. Two twenty, tops."

Hannah nodded.

"If it's okay," Frank said cautiously, "I should...."

"Throw down some silage. Sure. You want me to move the bins aside when they're full?"

"That would save me climbing up and down."

With the morning chores completed, they met at the outdoor pump, where they washed down their hands.

"Well, you have a free cow coming, Frank. That leaves nineteen. If you want, I'll sell you the whole herd for one seventy-five a head. It's up to you."

"That's a mighty generous offer." He paused. "Let me take it up with Norma."

His words stung Hannah. She turned away and took a long, slow breath. It wasn't just that Frank was considerate enough to include his wife in the decision – something most farming men simply wouldn't do. It was that his words reminded her she no longer had someone to turn to and ask for advice.

She sat on the edge of the concrete slab that supported the outdoor hand pump. "Could I trouble you to do me a small favor, Frank? Could you go into the kitchen and get my purse? It's on the desk, I'm sure. And while you're there, could you get the meatloaf and scalloped potatoes from the refrigerator and bring them out?"

"Sure. Anything else?"

"No. Not at the moment."

With Frank inside on the hunt, Hannah looked at the truck and smirked. "What are you looking at?"

Frank reappeared and sat next to Hannah, placing the items between them. He included a fork and glass of root beer in the inventory.

Midmorning Hannah began to wash the truck. She only intended to remove the months-long accumulation of dust acquired while stowed in the barn. When she rubbed the rag across the logo, *Whitman's Bread and Baked Goods*, the edges of the letters peeled away. With a dull putty knife, she was able to remove the hand-painted lettering without damaging the undercoat.

Hannah consulted the milking schedule. Dewey Hansen. From the milk house phone, Hannah called Dewey and asked if he could come an hour earlier than planned. It was not ideal, breaking the herd's routine, but Hannah wanted an uninterrupted evening.

The afternoon was spent as much as possible clearing the upper bay of equipment. She moved the cultivator, crimper and tedder into a side shed. She parked the harrow next to the bailer, between the corn crib and tool shed.

Larry and Jake showed up at five. They were high-school dropouts who formed a five-man country band, *CornDogs*. Simon and Gerald adored Larry and had fought for his attention whenever they visited the feed mill. He had an easy swagger, wore garish belt buckles, and shared Red Hots, which he kept in a snuff tin.

"We brought you a few bags of sorghum," Larry announced. "Seems they were just sitting in a corner of a boxcar, unclaimed."

"I'm not a charity case, Larry," Hannah said. "Take them back."

Larry ignored her demand. "I don't know why you requested Jake," he said, giving the bass player a sideway glance. "You said you needed muscle." Suddenly his mood grew somber. "I'm terribly sorry, Mrs. Mercer. It ain't right. There wasn't a better family in all of Kalb County."

"That's the nicest thing anybody's said to me these past few days," replied Hannah. A simple, heartfelt apology. Not laced in religious platitudes.

"What's on your mind?"

"I would like you to move all the furniture from the house into the barn."

An awkward silence settled on the trio. The boys exchanged looks, searching for an explanation that might make sense to them.

"You would like us to move all the furniture from the house into the barn?" parroted Jake.

Hannah nodded. "It might make for a good song!"

Larry was the first to laugh. Jake and Hannah joined in.

"Whatever you say."

Hannah pointed to the nearby wheelbarrow and Red Flyer Wagon. "We'll stack the dishes in here. Leave the clothes on their hangers and hang them on the clothes line or over the porch railing. The heavy stuff can be walked right in the barn. Leave the piano where it is."

Jake suggested they move the large, bulky items first.

The pair headed indoors, thinking Hannah would follow them. They paused in the kitchen, waiting. Any moment, they expected Hannah to enter and give them instructions. After several minutes, Larry tiptoed to the window and parted the curtains. Hannah was still seated by the water pump.

"I'm not sure she's coming in."

"What do you mean?"

"She's not moving."

"So what do we do?"

Puzzled, Larry circled the room and stopped at the door. He looked out a second time, then turned to Jake, thinking. "Why don't we start with the kitchen? When the wheelbarrow's full, let's see what happens."

They were both a little spooked about opening strange cupboards and pulling out stacks of plates, frying pans, saucers and cooking utensils.

"At any time, help yourself to food," Hannah instructed when they topped off the wheelbarrow. She grabbed the handles and headed toward the barn. By the time the Red Flyer was full, Hannah had returned with the empty wheelbarrow.

"What about the refrigerator? Do you want that?"

"Yes. But not the stove. It's gas."

For over three hours, Larry and Jake shuttled items to the barn, where Hannah arranged them into groupings. She plugged in the refrigerator, hung a wall clock on a hand-hewn post, attached the plugs of several floor lamps to an extension cord. She emptied the drawers and had two dressers placed inside the truck parked outside.

Larry grew more and more restless. His thoughts darkened. Was Hannah in the midst of a nervous breakdown? Was she contemplating suicide? Was she going to set fire to the house?

When Hannah declared an end to the operation, she and Jake sat on the sofa. Larry remained standing, chewing on a stem of dried hay. They waited for someone to break the silence, each in their own thoughts, serenaded by the smell of cattle.

"I would like you to have Horace's guitar and mandolin," Hannah announced.

"Mrs. Mercer," protested Larry, "now ain't the time to be giving away things that belonged to Horace."

"I know what I'm doing." She could see Larry didn't agree.

"They're worth keeping." added Jake, "You may find a use for them. In time."

"They belong to someone who understands them," Hannah said.

"The *CornDogs* are playing Saturday night at *The Stockyards*," volunteered Larry.

Hannah appeared not to have heard. "There's one more thing. In our ... in the bedroom ... in the south corner, there's a loose floorboard. Under it, you'll find a tin and two small wooden boxes."

"Yes, ma'am."

"I'd appreciate if you kept our business tonight to yourselves."

She paid the boys in cash.

After waving goodbye, Hannah climbed in the truck and backed it into the barn among all the household furnishings.

She got out and called for Five Paws, who scurried inside. Hannah closed and latched the barn doors. She opened the back doors to the truck, tossed some bedding and a pillow onto its floor, turned off all but one floor lamp and climbed inside. Five Paws jump onto the makeshift bed, nudged himself into the blankets and threw his body against hers.

The following day Hannah drove the car to Willmar, a town triple the size of Adele. The handsome General Store, on the corner of Franklin and Washington, was owned by Hugo Blackwell. A passionate student of the Bible, Hugo could recite a verse, foul or fair, for any occasion. His clipped, rectangular mustache conjured the ghost of a notorious German dictator.

"Mrs. Mercer! *Blessed are they who mourn for they shall have the habitat of God layed upon them and all their sorrows be vanity.*"

"Thank you for those kind words, Hugo. Could I use your facilities?"

Hugo pointed to a door leading to the storage area. "Through there." He looked over the rim of his glasses. "Only toilet paper, please, in the hopper!"

Rather than retire to the bathroom, Hannah began walking between the shelves examining various boxes, looking for shipping labels, and peeling them off if they seemed agreeable. She pushed up her sleeve, scribbling on her arm any company names that were stamped onto boxes. Kansas City and St. Louis seemed the most frequent addresses. She grabbed a handful of envelopes from a trash can. Stuffing her purse, Hannah wondered how Deacon Stahl would interpret her backroom raid. She returned to the store.

"Thank you, Mr. Blackwell."

A woman, standing across the counter from Hugo, dropped her shoulders. "I'm sorry for your loss."

Hannah frowned.

"Hugo was telling me about your circumstances."

"I don't think we've met," offered Hannah.

"I'm Vivian. Librarian at the Ruston County Branch. Just down the street."

"Nice to meet you, Vivian."

She wore a small hat, pleated at the side. Her blouse was cream colored with a double row of buttons down the front. Her tan, pressed slacks appeared new.

"We have a great deal of books," Vivian said, "that can be a comfort to people... in troubling times. If I can be of service, in any way, I'd be happy to assist you."

Hannah offered her a frosty smile, and instantly regretted it. There was a genuine tone to Vivian's sentiments, despite her bluntness.

"Thank you. Truly. I'll keep that in mind."

"Rejoice evermore," Hugo quoted. "Pray without ceasing."

Hannah began a tour of the store, noting how Hugo displayed his wares. She was distrustful of tags showing two prices, with a line drawn through the larger amount. It seemed clever to keep small items at eye level and place larger products on lower shelves. She imagined rearranging the sewing supplies to make a more captivating display.

Fortunately, Hugo held his post at the cash register and didn't cite any additional scripture.

Hannah purchased a hot plate and a small portable camping stove.

On the way home she stopped at a service station and purchased a foldout map of Missouri and a large, detailed map of St. Louis.

A few miles farther on, in the town of Ruston, she pulled into the parking lot of the Stock 'n Go Gun Shop. She didn't know the owner, Bernard, or his backup, a vicious-looking German Shepard named Bullet. Bernard was skeptical about Hannah's request; he pulled out the smallest rifle in stock.

"I never sold no lady no gun before," he sneered.

"If it weren't for menfolk having guns, I doubt I'd want one."

"You know how to shoot this?"

"I know how to work a sewing machine," countered Hannah. "It can't be all that hard."

"This is a powerful weapon."

"I would hope so. Otherwise I'd be throwing money in the wind, wouldn't I?"

Bernard nervously twisted his caterpillar eyebrows. "It just don't seem right, a proper woman like you toting a gun."

Hannah glimpsed at Bernard's left hand. "What are you afraid of? That I'll form a lady's rifle team and your wife will join?"

The barb didn't register well with Bernard. "I was thinking the metalwork could use some more fanciful etching. Something pretty. Lacy. Feminine-like. But I'm not so sure that suits you."

Hannah ignored his retort. She glanced at Bullet and decided to purchase the Winchester.

Back at the farm, Hannah threw open the barn doors. Light filtered through the dust. Below, she could hear the occasional click of the electric fence monitor, signifying its vigilance. She found a pair of sawhorses the height of the truck bed and laid several planks across them. After clamping them in place, she pushed the dresser that was once in her bedroom from inside the truck onto the planks. She climbed the ladder to the hay mow and readjusted the block and tackle lashed to the beam. Wrapping a rope around the dresser and tying the ends with a bowline knot, she used the pulley to raise the dresser several inches. She sawed off the legs, lowered the dresser and pushed it back into the truck. Using small angle irons and a handful of screws, she attached the dresser to the truck's side frame.

She turned on the radio and found Horace's favorite station, the only option that featured classical music.

Hannah pulled the drawers from the second dresser, removed the handles and stacked the drawers on their sides, creating a menagerie of shelves and dividers.

Most of the donated food, beginning to sour, was tossed in the garden compost. Preparing herself a plate of cheese, pickles and dried apricots, Hannah turned the radio dial to 98.6 and sat down for dinner. The announcer was predicting a late-evening thunderstorm. Once again Germany was in the news. The Berlin Wall, begun just a few months earlier, in August 1961, was the scene of another daring escape. Olga Segler had jumped from her window in the eastern sector into a net held by West Berlin firefighters. Although she survived the fall, she suffered a heart attack and died. Olga was eighty years old. For dessert, Hannah finished the last of Naomi's banana ice cream, imagining the scene that played out in Berlin.

She dumped the contents of her purse on the desk and began to organize and study the shipping labels. Earlier, driving away from Hugo's general store, while shifting into second gear, Hannah had decided to limit her search to St. Louis. Now, looking through the receipts, Hugo appeared to do business primarily with three distributors in the city. Consulting the city map, Hannah selected *Cantor's Warehouse and Supply Center.* It was on the northern border of St. Louis, the shortest distance from Adele.

She unfolded the map of Missouri. Using embroidery thread, she calculated a distance of fifty miles. She wrapped the thread around the point of a pencil, placed the other end on Adele and with this handmade compass drew a circle around her home town. Using a collection of colored pencils she began to map out several routes, each starting and ending in Adele, reaching into outlying counties, never crossing the leaded circumference.

The wind began picking up.

Several times Hannah erased portions of a route to reimagine it.

She noticed the drop in air pressure and smelled the charged air, announcing the approaching front. Five Paws paced the floor, pausing from time to time to listen to the creaking rafters. Hannah ran outdoors to make certain the gate to the barnyard was open. Most of the cows had already taken shelter under the protective roof.

She thought of her husband and sons, their graves under the sycamore, about to face the rainstorm.

It was impossible to do any further work that night. Hannah simply sat at the back of the truck, the door open, her feet dangling, not touching the floor, listening to the sound of rain on the tin roof.

Hannah awoke before sunrise. The cows had returned to the meadow to graze on fescue before milking. Only a few branches had broken free and were scattered on the lawn. She gathered them together and threw them on a burn pile. She collected soap, fresh clothes and gave herself a sponge bath in the milk house.

Jesse Sommers was scheduled to supervise the milking that morning. More than a week had passed since Hannah inspected the garden, so she decided to harvest any forgotten vegetables and send them home with Jesse. She was filling a second basket of tomatoes when Larry drove up.

"I never did check them spark plugs the other day," he said, leaning out the window.

"Shouldn't you be at work?" Hannah asked, wiping her hands on the sides of her dress.

Larry winked. "I was granted parole for the day. Good behavior."

They walked, side by side, to the tool shed.

"Anything belonging to Horace to make the job easier, help yourself."

"While I'm at it, I thought an oil change would be in order."

On their way to the barn, Hannah brushed back her hair. The sharp, earth-oil scent of tomatoes on her hand caused her to stop. Normally the tomatoes would be cooked down, pressed through a colander and reheated with sugar and spices. Then the sauce would be poured in Mason jars, cooked in a hot water bath and stored in the basement pantry for her family.

Hannah's momentary break didn't go unnoticed by Larry.

"Are you okay, Mrs. Mercer?"

Hannah smiled weakly. "I'm going to have to learn to lie, Larry," she said.

"Why's that?"

"To spare everyone... and myself."

Larry choose not to press her.

The following day Hannah drove an exquisitely-tuned, wholly-agreeable truck to St. Louis. *Cantor's Warehouse and Supply Center.* Hannah cruised Filmore Drive slowly, peering left and right, for the depository. It was set back from the street; a blue awning framed a single door to the office.

Hannah backed the jaunty Metro van into a parking slot and engaged the parking brake. Not since high school had she dared to wear a trace of forbidden lipstick, but she applied a blushingly-red coat. She sat for a moment, clutching her purse, gathering her wits.

The receptionist was seated behind a low desk, with a container of rubber cement, gluing eraser caps onto the heads of used, bald pencils. She looked up.

"You're lost, aren't you?"

"No. I'm here," replied Hannah.

Without malice, the receptionist stroked the side of her lip with her forefinger and said, "There's a lady's room down the hall."

Hannah attempted a smile and shrugged her shoulders. "Oh, who's kidding who?" She opened her purse, removed a handkerchief and wiped off the lipstick. She tucked the handkerchief back in her purse and snapped it shut, saying, "Am I myself?"

The receptionist was pleasantly amused. "I don't know. Who are you?"

"Hannah. Hannah Mercer. My name is Hannah Mercer."

The receptionist rose and extended her hand. "I'm Wanda. Wanda Garrick."

"I'm here to purchase a variety of items, although I'm not familiar with your company and don't know what you sell or the cost of your goods."

"Do you have a license?"

"I wouldn't drive the whole way from Adele, for three hours, without a license."

"No. A business license."

"I need permission to buy and sell things?"

"Yes. You do."

"Can you give me one?"

"I'm afraid not. You must apply for one. Most likely in the county where you live."

"You can't sell me anything? Even if I pay cash."

"I'm sorry. It's the law. *Cantor's* is a wholesale operation. We can't open an account without a license."

"Well, okay, then," Hannah said.

Wanda noticed the defeat in Hannah's eyes. "I suspect you want a retail license. Giving you permission to buy and resell merchandise."

"Yes. Exactly! But I don't understand. Why?"

"It's a business transaction. The government wants to make sure you collect and pay sales tax." Not a fan of government regulations, Wanda snorted.

Hannah turned and looked out the window, at the empty truck.

Wanda checked the clock on the wall.

"Have you had lunch? It's nearly noon. Mollie's Diner is just a five-minute walk down the road."

"Oh, that would be nice," admitted Hannah. "I would love some coffee."

"Let me get a catalog, so you can get a sense of what we sell. Everything is sold in bulk, you know."

"I assumed," nodded Hannah. "I was hoping."

Wanda walked to the windows, closed the blinds and flipped the Open-Closed sign on the door.

"Do you have a sample license I could see?" Hannah asked.

"We keep copies on file. Technically, the client must give permission to release any documents."

"I understand. Of course."

Wanda considered. "Mr. Henderson passed away recently," she said to herself. "We're in the process of closing his account." She returned to her desk, extracted a ring of keys and opened the middle drawer of a filing cabinet. She flipped through a row of tabs and slipped out a folder. Wanda held up the file and gave it a flick. "I doubt Mr. Henderson minds."

Over lunch, flashing her knife and fork like a conductor before a symphony of meatballs, mashed potatoes and lima beans, Wanda explained her lifelong desire: to become a stunt pilot and perform aerial feats, flying under bridges, through gorges, buzzing tornadoes. She paused and massaged her coffee mug with the sides of her hands. "I hate my job. I hate St. Louis. I hate my life."

Hannah looked on her kindly, without saying a word.

A second later, Wanda apologized. "You know I don't mean that." She stiffened her spine and slapped the table. "You drove three hours. We can't send you home empty-handed." She folded the license and handed it to Hannah. "We'll work something out, Mr. Henderson."

Back at the warehouse, Wanda introduced Hannah to Katherine, a fork lift operator. For the next hour, without regard to company regulations, Katherine zipped Hannah along the corridors, selecting merchandize, stacking boxes on flats and transporting them to the Metro, in its proud, new position at the end of the loading dock.

Wanda tallied the invoice, collected Hannah's payment and followed her to the loading dock.

"Next time you'll have a proper license," she cautioned.

It was dusk when Hannah drove down the lane, returning to the farm. The only light was a whisper under the porch, by the front door. Before parking the truck, she stopped, turned off the engine and began walking to the water pump. A quietness had settled over the farm, a stillness so complete, she paused, almost alarmed at the breathless air. What was it? Why the change? There was no rustle in the grass, no quiet shifting in the barnyard. And then she knew. The cattle were gone.

She found the note clipped to the screen door with a clothespin.

> *I accepted your offer. Norma's nephew from Topeka was passing through and helped move the herd this afternoon. He's much better at handling cattle than me. I hope that's okay.*

"I acted too soon," whispered Hannah, flushed with a rising sense of panic. "What was I thinking?" She primed the pump handle and drank a handful of water. It was not going to be an easy night.

*****

*****

Just outside Adele, on the road to Willmar, Nathan Proctor had purchased a parcel of land from his cousin, Matthew Proctor, and had built a fourteen-unit motor lodge. Entrances to each room, framed by a pair of windows, created an uninterrupted rhythm on three walls that faced the central parking lot. A lobby was tacked on the end of the north arm of the lodge. Nathan, a bachelor, claimed the room nearest the lobby, calling it home. Later, Nathan would add two small, independent cabins to his empire. The most distinctive feature was its sign – a glorious, internally-lit triangle mounted on two poles embedded in a brick planter – that promised comfortable beds, free coffee and color television.

From the outset, the lodge was not a wise investment. Few people sought refuge in this corner of Missouri. The Interstate, miles away, was not a conduit for business.

To supplement his income, Nathan went to night school and became an auctioneer. To advertise his hotel, he hosted a one-hour radio show each week entitled *Kalb County Speaks* and interviewed local celebrities. Both were wise decisions. Nathan had a lovely baritone voice.

Hannah paid Nathan a visit.

"I intend to sell the farm."

Nathan adjusted his bow tie. "There's been talk of that."

"Will you oversee the sale?"

"Mrs. Mercer," appealed Nathan, "there's no rush, is there? Can't you employ a hired hand to mind the farm?"

"It belonged to my husband. It is no longer a farm."

"It's an excellent parcel of land. Consider it an investment."

"I can't argue, Nathan. The land is lovely."

Nathan shifted in his chair.

"Six percent," Hannah proposed. "That's your share. It's more than fair."

"Fair!" gasped Nathan. "It's sinful. Nobody takes a six percent commission."

"Everything goes. All but one half acre. The land where Horace and my boys are buried. That I'm keeping for myself."

"If I may ..." Nathan ventured, "where do you plan to go?"

Hannah smiled, the smile of someone entertaining an unusual proposition.

"Would I be able to park my truck here, out of the way, perhaps out back?"

Nathan waited for clarification.

"I noticed several outdoor outlets by the laundry."

Nathan nodded, knowingly.

"And if I could purchase electricity from time to time. When needed."

"Why not rent a room? I could draw up a lease. One of the cottages, perhaps."

"I'll consider that. But, at the moment, just a place to park. ... I don't expect I'll need much electricity."

"I'm not familiar with the truck you keep mentioning. Is it large? Loud? Does it leak oil? Will its tires kick up gravel?"

"Why don't you come to the farm," urged Hannah. "I'll show you."

*****

*****

A sign announcing the sale of the Mercer Farm was posted at the end of the driveway. Flyers were distributed to local businesses. An ad ran in the *Willmar Gazette.*

Over several days, Hannah created a stencil and, using chalk, transferred the design to each side of the Metro. Slowly, with great care, she filled in the letters with gold paint: *Hannah's Goods and Effects.*

Nathan employed a team of helpers to sort and box Horace's tools, polish the equipment, harvest the last of the year's crops.

Hannah built a rack of angled dowels for spools of thread. She bundled bolts of fabric and strapped them in with leather belts. Packets of seeds, jars of buttons, canisters of spices were sorted and stacked.

Nathan's team applied a fresh coat of paint to the milk house. They filled the ruts in the driveway. The roof on the north side of the house was re-shingled.

Drawers were labeled and filled with light bulbs, laundry soap, toothpaste, Brillo pads. Cupboards were lined with bottles of cough syrup, vapor rubs, eardrops. Using a bookcase as a base, she constructed a fold-down bed. She installed the armoire, filled it with her clothes and built a false floor where she hid the lockbox that had been stored in her bedroom. She tucked a chamber pot inside a hamper in a corner of the truck. A small cupboard, with pierced tin doors, built for holding pies, was filled with books. A scale was hung from the roof.

"What would you like me to do with the piano?" asked Nathan?

Hannah pondered for a moment. "Is there room in the lobby of your hotel?"

Nathan did a quick inventory. "I could find a place, I suppose."

"Wonderful!"

"And the canned goods in the basement?" Before Hannah could answer, he added, "I can't sell them. And it's unlikely an agency will accept them. Charities don't take food prepared at home, only commercial products. It's a safety thing."

Hannah seemed offended.

"But if you find someone who wants the lot, I'll have my boys deliver them."

"And you? Will you take a few jars of jam and pickled beans? Or do you suspect they're poisoned, too?"

During the auction, Hannah paid little attention to the proceedings. She walked along the pasture fence and sat by the small dam hugging the creek. Time was passed on the hillside, under the sycamore. Below, Nathan could be heard encouraging buyers to ratchet up their bids. His voice, lyrical and soothing as a nocturne played by Horace, cast a hypnotic spell over the crowd.

Hannah decided she would send a portion of the sales to Horace's parents, living in an old folks home in Iowa City.

When the bargaining ended and everyone had departed, Hannah climbed into the Metro with Five Paws and drove down the lane. She stopped at the road, got out, passed in front of the truck and paused by the mailbox. Slowly, she removed the small, reflective, stick-on letters: *Horace and Hannah Mercer.*

*****

*****

Hannah had contrived eight routes, making rounds on Monday, Tuesday, Thursday and Friday, retracing each circuit every other week. Wednesdays were reserved for trips to St. Louis, to restock her inventory, if needed. Most people were intrigued by a traveling store and welcomed Hannah's visits.

After several weeks, she no longer needed to consult her maps or refer to the list of addresses to pass by.

*****

*****

In mid-November, Hannah made her second trip to St. Louis.

"It's a very odd-looking license," Wanda said, scrutinizing the document. She tugged on the left sleeve of her sweater.

"What do you mean?"

"It looks more like a diploma or scouting certificate," Wanda mused, turning over the paper.

"Could it appear different because I don't have a traditional business? My store, after all, is a truck."

The answer seemed to satisfy Wanda, who placed the paper on top of the filing cabinet, while keeping the edge of her sleeve pinched in the palm of her left hand.

"If I may, I would like to treat you to lunch at Mollie's Diner, Hannah said.

"There's no need to do that, Mrs. Mercer."

"I insist," pressed Hannah. "Unless you have other plans."

Preparing to leave, Wanda turned her back to Hannah, who noticed how awkwardly she slipped into her gray herringbone coat.

Wanda ordered a bowl of ham and bean soup. Hannah selected waffles and creamed chipped beef. Waiting for a moment for Wanda to look away, Hannah pushed her fork off the right side of the table. As Wanda reached to pick up the utensil, Hannah leaned over. Stretching to grasp the fork, the sleeve on Wanda's arm rode up. Hannah saw a bandage wrapped around her wrist.

After the waitress had cleared the plates and Hannah asked for a second cup of coffee, she pulled her chair forward and lowered her voice.

"I am a thirty-six-year old child. When I came to *Cantor's* I had no experience in running a business. You made it possible. You got me started. I'm sure, along the way, I'll have many questions. So, I'll be looking to you for advice, asking for your opinion. Is that okay? Are you willing to help?"

Wanda nodded. Under the table she rested her right hand over her left wrist. Her eyes were misty. "We have a few items that have been hard to move," she ventured. "I can offer them at a nice discount."

"Sounds wonderful! And when you become a pilot," added Hannah, "I hope you'll introduce me to your replacement!"

"Thirty-six?" repeated Wanda.

Hannah could think of no fitting response.

"I'm twenty-five," Wanda volunteered.

"At your age," Hannah said, "I still hadn't met my husband."

Wanda decided to have dessert and hailed the waitress.

"Does *Cantor's* have any books?" asked Hannah.

"Cookbooks, mainly. And inspirational garbage. You know. Devotionals. Angels and halos and sad-eyed Jesus offering salvation. Oh, sorry. I hope I didn't offend you."

"Not at all."

"But you're Mennonite. So, I'm guessing anything Jesus can be a bit...." She offered a two-hand shimmy. "Weird."

Hannah shrugged.

"I'll try to keep all swearing to a minimum," promised Wanda. "What kind of books?"

"Story books, mainly."

"Like novels?"

"Yes, I suppose. And books for children."

Wanda's face lit up. "I have books at home I'll sell you. And I know a couple of good second-hand bookshops."

"Yes. They needn't be new. Used books would be fine, I'm sure."

"I'll see what I can round up by your next visit. Did you ever read *Look Homeward, Angel*?"

"No. Who's it by?"

"Thomas Wolfe. At first I was a bit creeped by the title. But, no, it's good."

With a load of fresh supplies, Hannah headed back to Adele.

That evening, while Hannah was sorting through boxes, Nathan knocked on the door of the Metro.

"They're showing *It's a Wonderful Life* tonight. Would you like to watch it with me?"

Hannah appeared confused.

"You don't know *It's a Wonderful Life*? Jimmy Stewart. Frank Capra. George Bailey."

Hannah shook her head. "We didn't have television growing up," she admitted.

"Come to think of it, there wasn't one at the auction."

"The church frowns upon such worldly possessions. Horace found other ways to fill his time."

"Normally they don't broadcast the movie until after Thanksgiving. I guess Christmas is coming early this year."

Hannah considered his proposition, taking note of the jobs before her.

"I purchased a new Zenith," Nathan explained. "It's just what the lobby needed. The reception is great."

"Alright," consented Hannah. Instinctively she wanted to call out, "Simon. Gerald. Do you want to watch *It's a Wonderful Life*?"

*****

*****

Early December, in the midst of a snow-globe storm, Hannah veered off the road and slid into a shallow ditch. For twenty minutes she rocked the van back and forth, pausing to shovel snow from under the wheel well. During the ordeal, only one car drove past. Hannah was certain Deacon Stahl was behind the wheel.

A bearded tractor driver, pulling a manure spreader, stopped to assist Hannah. Rather than unhook the spreader, the driver attached a chain to it and the Metro. As the van was nudged back on the road, the rotors of the spreader began spinning and kicked up fresh manure, splattering the windshield and hood.

Without telling anyone, Hannah drove directly to the interstate and headed south.

*****

*****

In March of the following year, Hannah returned and resumed her rounds.

There was one change in the display of her wares that spring of 1962. The section devoted to books had been expanded to include a second cupboard, filled to capacity. Soon, Hannah pledged, on a free day she was going to pay Vivian, the librarian in Willmar, a visit.

On a Thursday route, as Hannah crested a hill, she noticed, ahead, a woman seated in a chair by the side of the road, next to a mailbox. The address was a familiar one. As Hannah approached, the woman stepped into the road and began waving her hands. Hannah's fears were realized; it was Naomi Stahl. Hannah brought the van to a stop. Standing at road's edge, Naomi tapped on the window and motioned for Hannah to open the passenger door.

Hannah shook her head.

Naomi stepped on the running board and shouted through the window. "Why don't you include me in your itinerary? Are we no longer friends?"

Hannah continued to stare straight ahead.

"Hannah! Answer me! Have you forgotten my name?"

"I haven't forgotten your name, Naomi," answered Hannah, still refusing to look at the Deacon's wife. She released her foot on the brake and the truck began drifting forward.

"Hannah, open the door!"

"I know where I'm not welcome."

"You're being unfair!" cried Naomi.

Hannah pressed down on the brake, leaned across the seat and unlatched the door handle.

Naomi climbed in.

Still refusing to look at her passenger, Hannah turned the truck around.

"Where are you going?"

Hannah gunned it. The Metro, kicked in the ribs, began to gallop.

"Slow down, Hannah, please!" pleaded Naomi.

At the third intersection, Hannah turned right, the tires screeching as she negotiated the turn. One more turn, and she brought the van to a stop in the parking lot of Creekside Mennonite Church.

Both were breathing heavily.

"You see that!"

"Of course, I do, Hannah. Don't be silly."

"When Creekside burned down eight years ago, my husband helped rebuild its walls. He came with a paint brush and a box of tools and a ready hand, and nobody said, 'Are you a member of this church!'"

"Everyone remembers. He was tireless."

"They accepted his help, without ever questioning his faith."

Naomi understood. "I'm sorry," she said.

Hannah leaned against the steering wheel, resting her forehead against her crossed forearms.

"Don't mistake me for Eli," Naomi whispered. She reached over and touched Hannah on the shoulder.

Hannah managed a small nod of her head.

"You're missed at church."

"I was in Florida for the winter."

"Florida?" Naomi said wistfully. "I would love to go to Florida. Was it lovely?"

"It is quite nice. Yes."

"I've heard so much about your shop. *Hannah's Goods and Effects*. May I have a look?"

"Please. Help yourself. I'm going to step outside and have a smoke."

Naomi was unable to contain her shock, but quickly replaced it with a sly smile. "Aren't you the wicked one." She slipped between the driver and passenger seat, parted the curtains and entered the cargo hold.

Hannah opened the back door, giving Naomi light, and settled down on the opposite side of the road.

When Naomi joined Hannah, she held a small collection of books in her arms, including *Look Homeward, Angel* by Thomas Wolfe. At Wanda's recommendation, Hannah had purchased and read the book in Florida.

"I would like to purchase these, please."

While tallying the prices, written lightly in pencil on the front inside cover, Hannah asked, "Do you know the story of *Madame Bovary*?"

"No."

"I don't think you'd find her in a pew at Creekside."

"Then I may find the book very much to my liking," replied Naomi, sitting next to Hannah. She spread her knees, hiked up her skirt a few inches. "I'd love to have a cigarette with you."

For several minutes they sat in silence, wrapped in a small cloud of smoke. Naomi was the first to speak. "This is so wrong."

Later that day, Hannah called on the Leichty family. What little she knew about them she'd learned from Naomi, who found Mr. Leichty elusively handsome, an ideal convert for Creekside Mennonite Church.

"You're a Godsend," Frances exclaimed, "I ran out of yellow thread sewing a dress for Darla."

She purchased two spools of thread, a yard of trim, shoe polish and a glass-studded barrette. "How many more customers will you see today?"

"Just a handful," replied Hannah. "I'm at the end of my round."

"Why don't you come for dinner? After you're through?"

"That would be lovely. Thank you."

"I can't promise anything fancy. But Quincy tells me the hams are fully cured."

"I'm sure it'll be delicious."

Hannah was seated in the living room, waiting for Frances to announce dinner when Darla appeared, looking around the deep, beveled door frame.

"Hello," Hannah said. "Are you Darla?"

The girl, who looked about ten years old, quickly withdrew.

Hannah kept eyeing the doorway, waiting for Darla to reappear, but the child had vanished.

At the dinner table, Hannah got her first, good look at the Leichty family. Quincy was small-boned, almost delicate. He had iridescent eyes, a simple nose and narrow but shapely lips. Their son, Adam, had a sweet, unassuming face showered with freckles. Darla had inherited her father's eyes, but they were deeper and richer in tone. She gestured rather than spoke her intentions. Frances seemed a model of aristocratic breeding: high cheekbones, arched brows and a serene temperament.

Only when Frances responded with a sweeping, upward-palm gesture towards her daughter did Hannah realize Darla was deaf.

Hannah looked across the table at the young girl. Frances noticed the exchange and assumed there might be a shadow of pity in Hannah's eyes. But there was none, only admiration.

Adam proclaimed, "She reads lips."

"That's true," chimed in Frances. "When that fails, we have our signs. And, there's always paper and a pencil."

When Frances rose to get dessert, Darla caught her mother's attention with a slight gesture. Frances nodded. With a small wave, Darla excused herself. When she returned she offered a paper to Hannah. It was a drawing of the Metro.

"Oh, my goodness!" exclaimed Hannah, her hand cupping her cheek. "Would you look at that! It's as honest as a photograph. No, it's better than a photograph!"

Darla returned to her seat, smiling, her hands pressed together in a prayerful position.

Hannah beamed. "Beautiful" she mouthed. "Just beautiful."

"She means for you to have it," Frances said.

*****

*****

Soon, dinner with the Leichty family became a bi-weekly affair.

"Whenever you're set to arrive, Darla spends the entire evening before deciding which drawings to show you," acknowledged Frances.

With summer approaching Darla convinced her mother, reluctantly, to question Hannah. They were seated on the lawn. Nearby, Quincy and Adam were pitching quoits.

"Darla," Frances began, taking a broken breath, "thinks you're the most traveled woman in the world."

"The world?" laughed Hannah. "I haven't traveled much farther than St. Louis. It's true, as a girl I went to Denver. That's about as far as it goes."

Darla was clearly puzzled. She raised her hands and pantomimed six gestures that said: I ... think ... sun ... water ... swim ... palm trees.

"Oh! Florida!" confessed Hannah. "How could I forget? My goodness, I was just there a few months ago!" She fell silent for a moment.

"If I'm being forward, please tell me," interrupted Frances.

"No. No. What's on your mind?"

"It's more ... what's on Darla's mind."

Hannah laughed and reached over to pat an anxious Darla on her forearm.

"Next time you go to St. Louis, would you be willing to have Darla accompany you? As a guest?"

Hannah tapped herself, made a small circle over her heart and pointed to Darla, saying. "I think that's a wonderful idea. I would enjoy the company."

Relieved, Frances settled back in her chair.

"When were you thinking?"

"School's out in June. So, after that. Whatever suits your schedule."

*****

All that summer Darla frequently accompanied Hannah on her rounds. When they came to a gated farm, Darla would jump out, open the gate and flag Hannah through. Mid-afternoon, on hot days, they would often stop at a country store and treat themselves to ice cream, sitting on the ground in the shade, leaning against the truck. Five Paws, confined to the Metro, cried pitifully, hoping for a lick of their treats.

The abandoned Shenk Farm, reached by crossing a small bridge on the property, became a favorite setting. The meadow was a perfect place to park the Metro, scoop water from the shallow stream and wash the van.

Late in the summer, as gardens in bountiful excess charmed their caregivers, Hannah paused to visit her family's gravesite. Darla intended to remain in the truck with Five Paws, but Hannah invited her partner to step outside. After sitting against *Periscope* for a spell, Hannah rose and walked along the crest of the hill. She observed the farm below. A woman was removing wash from the line. A young girl on a swing flashed in and out of the shadows. Darla collected her sketch pad and pencils from the van. Returning to the embrace of *Periscope*, Hannah was joined by her former neighbor.

"Frank!" exclaimed Hannah.

"Norma saw your truck. She sent me up for scouring pads."

"You know Quincy and Frances Leichty. This is Darla, their oldest."

Frank tipped his hat.

"Sit down. I want to hear about your new neighbors," urged Hannah.

"There ain't a whole lot to say. They come from Nebraska, where they ran a roofing business."

"Are they smart about tending the roses?"

"I wouldn't know. It's not like it was... when I would visit Horace and you...."

"How is Norma?"

"It's hard to say. There are good days and bad days."

"And the cows? Are they behaving?"

"Oh yes. That was a good investment."

"Do you think they would recognize me?"

"Who can say? I reckon they would."

A long silence passed between them.

"Well," Frank said, "standing here isn't getting the hay turned."

Darla approached Hannah, offering her the drawing she had just completed. Hannah indicated Darla should offer the drawing to Frank.

"Well, I'll be. Truly. That is me, so far as I can tell." He held it up for Hannah to see, "Is that me, Hannah?"

"It surely is. Darla is a very talented artist."

Frank attempted to hand back the drawing.

"No, it's yours. That's the way Darla operates."

Pleased, Frank reached in his pocket. He offered Darla a coin. She accepted then offered the coin to Hannah.

"No. No," Hannah said, shaking her head. "It's yours!"

After Frank departed, Darla handed Hannah a note.

He's in love with you.

Hannah was taken aback by Darla's announcement. "Love? What do you know of Love?" she scoffed, tearing the note from the pad and crumpling it.

*****

*****

When winter showed its full, fierce face, Hannah once more retreated to Florida.

Returning in the spring of 1963, Hannah was surprised to learn the Shenk Farm had been sold. She decided to introduce herself to the new owners.

The bridge grumbled disagreeably as Hannah drove over the aging planks. A couple paused to observe the approaching truck. The woman was turning over soil in the garden. A man of oak-tree stature was reinforcing the gate to the pasture. They walked over to Hannah as she stepped from the van. Until now, Kalb County was no home to black farmers.

"Hello."

Hannah smiled.

"I'm LeRoy Williams. This is my wife, Ethel."

"I'm glad to finally see the farm in good hands. I'm Hannah."

"It needs a whole lot of tending," admitted Ethel.

"Our boy, Sam, is around somewhere, probably on the hunt for snakes."

"I operate a simple country store on wheels," Hannah explained. "Should you be interested, every two weeks I'll pay a visit. If you like, I can show you what I have to offer."

The couple observed the neatly-arranged merchandise, with attractive labels by Darla.

With his fingers, LeRoy tapped out a smart rhythm on the edge of a shelf, then spun around. "What I need most is a guitar," he said in half-seriousness.

Ethel elaborated. "His got crushed in the move."

That night Hannah wandered into the hotel lobby and sat by the fireplace, resting her feet on the fieldstone base.

Nathan was mesmerized by Walter Cronkite recounting the day's news.

"Jackie Kennedy is pregnant," Nathan reported during a commercial break. "A Christmas present for Caroline and John Jr.," he added.

"Nathan, who bought Horace's guitar?"

"King is still in jail in Alabama. That was Larry, wasn't it? And he bought the mandolin, too, I think. Solitary confinement. That's excessive."

When Hannah asked for Larry at the feed mill, she was told he no longer worked there.

"Do you know where he is now?"

"Mrs. Mercer, Larry is a dropout," Hannah was told. "Little League. High school. Any job that pays a decent wage. He just walks away, like some toothless tomcat, remorseless and carefree. Good luck finding him."

She drove to *The Stockyards*. At three in the afternoon the nightclub still hadn't kicked into first gear.

"Yeah. Larry. He'll be playing here Saturday night with the boys."

"The *CornDogs*," Hannah said, jogging her memory.

"No. Dropped out. Formed a new group, *PepperChips*."

Hannah looked around.

"First time?"

Hannah nodded.

"Would you care for a drink?"

"No, thank you."

"You're one of those Mennonites?"

"I am a member…."

"Dang. What is it with you folks? Even Jesus rocked the brew."

*****

*****

Larry was in the middle of an original song, *Spilling Beans*, when he spotted Hannah in the crowd. He flagged the band to stop. "Ladies and gentlemen. I have just been treated to the sight of an old friend in the audience. You may know her as a traveling saleslady. I know her as a writer of songs." He called across the room, to the bartender, "Sonny, drinks to Miss Hannah Mercer, Queen of Kalb County!"

During a break between sets, Larry snagged a chair from backstage and sat next to Hannah.

"How are you? I hope I didn't embarrass you too much. What did Sonny bring you?"

"I'm not sure. Beer?"

Larry took a sip. "You're not going to try it?"

"Thanks. No."

"You need a lady's drink. Let me see what I can do." He rose and made his way to the bar. In a few minutes he returned and cautiously, reverently, placed a drink on the table. "Sloe gin fizz."

Hannah obliged. She took a shallow sip.

"Don't be shy. Give it a good kiss."

Hannah blushed.

"I was wondering if you still have Horace's guitar?" she asked cautiously.

"I do."

"Would you be willing to sell it back to me?"

A huge grin spread across the face of Larry. "I told you! Didn't I tell you!" he said without malice or pride. "Damn. Had I known, I would have brought it with me."

*****

*****

On Sunday evening, as Hannah was trimming the wicks and refueling the kerosene lanterns, there was a knock on the back door of the Metro.

"Frank called," Nathan announced. He handed Hannah a discarded hotel receipt with the phone number. "He'd like to hear from you."

Hannah relayed Frank's message to Darla. "He'd like you to draw a picture of his wife, Norma, to accompany the one you made of him."

The following Saturday Norma reluctantly posed for Darla. She sat, rather formally, in a narrow Victorian chair with brocaded fabric. Hannah observed that Norma had lost weight and her pale skin had a slight gray flush.

Frank could be heard on the porch, husking sweet corn and removing the silk with a nylon bristle brush. Laverne, recently hired by Frank to assist with household work, was in the kitchen blanching the ears, cutting off the kernels and packing them in plastic bags for freezing.

Darla instantly realized the error of Norma's choice. She looked to Hannah for guidance, writing her a short note.

"Darla thinks there may be a better pose," Hannah told Norma. "Perhaps another chair. A different room. Or outdoors."

Norma rose. Hannah and Darla followed her as they walked through the kitchen then circled back to the living room to survey its options. Darla was unconvinced; she led them outdoors. Norma was asked to sit on the edge of the porch, next to the railing.

At Darla's urging, Hannah said, "Darla would like you to remove your shoes and pretend to polish one."

Seeing the care Norma had fawned on her shoes, Hannah understood.

Norma relaxed. Darla nodded, took a seat and began sketching.

Retreating to the van, Hannah busied herself, making a list for her next trip to St. Louis. There was a timid knock on the panel by the open door. It was Laverne.

"Would you like help in the kitchen?"

Laverne shook her head. "May I come in?"

"Of course, of course."

Laverne stepped inside and looked around, unsure whether to proceed or not.

"How can I help?"

"Do you have any products for women?"

Given Laverne's reticence, Hannah made a seasoned guess. "Would you like sanitary napkins?"

"No."

"I don't sell makeup. And I stopped carrying perfume."

Laverne glanced about, appearing to be confined in a cage. "Women products that ...."

"Are you pregnant?" ventured Hannah.

Laverne nodded.

"I see."

"Please don't tell anyone, Mrs. Mercer."

Hannah stiffened. She looked over Laverne's shoulder, past the open door.

"No! Not Frank!"

Though Hannah tried to hide it, Laverne saw her give a visible sigh of relief.

"I can't have the child!" cried Laverne. "I just can't."

From her past, Hannah heard a familiar refrain:

> *Have we trials and temptations? Is there trouble everywhere?*

"I understand," she lied.

> *Take it to the Lord in prayer.*

"Well, you can't.... You mustn't attempt anything on your own!"

"I'm desperate, Mrs. Mercer!"

Hannah clenched her fist. "We can't have you crying. You can't go back in there, looking undone."

Take it to the Lord....

"I have a friend in St. Louis. Perhaps she knows a doctor who can help. Next time I see her, I'll inquire. In the meantime, do nothing! Do you hear me! Nothing! This is not something you should attempt on your own!"

"I promise, Mrs. Mercer. Thank you."

She backed to the door, slowly turned and stepped down. Outside, she paused and looked over her shoulder. "Thank you, Hannah."

Hannah stood in the doorway, overcome with pity, overcome with anger. She thought of her sons, Simon and Gerald. How could Laverne contemplate such an act? Didn't she have children dear to her? Cousins? Nephews? Nieces?

When Hannah returned to the porch, Laverne was serving iced tea. Having completed her sketch, Darla excused herself and went searching for other scenes to draw. Half an hour later, as Hannah and Norma were finishing some freshly fried corn fritters drizzled with molasses, Darla returned and handed Frank several drawings.

Later that night, lying in bed, Hannah would ask herself, "Why was I so quick to judge Laverne? Why didn't I think to condemn the man who laid with her?"

*****

*****

When Hannah paid LeRoy and Ethel a second visit, Darla accompanied her. Approaching the house, they saw Sam seated on an upended chicken coop, wrapped in a cloth, getting a haircut. Ethel brushed hair clippings from his shoulders and waved. LeRoy rounded a corner of the house, paintbrush in hand.

"I found something you might like," Hannah announced, sliding from the driver's seat.

LeRoy rested his brush on the porch railing, pulled a rag out of his back pocket and began wiping his hands.

It was Hannah's custom to let customers meet her at the Metro, but today she unreservedly joined the Williams family on their porch.

Meanwhile, Darla had retrieved Hannah's gift from the back of the truck. She walked across the weed-choked lawn, carrying Horace's guitar.

Ethel joined LeRoy to stand by her husband.

Hannah whispered, "She may not hear but she understands everything."

Darla handed LeRoy the guitar, but she was watching Sam, still imprisoned in his fabric cone.

"I can't afford this," LeRoy said, looking down at the guitar, recognizing its craftsmanship.

"Do you see a price tag?" asked Hannah.

"No."

"Well, then, I suppose it's free."

"Free?" LeRoy repeated, mockingly.

"Yes. It's yours. Free."

"I can't accept this, Miss Mercer."

"I know what music can do for a man," replied Hannah. "It's yours now. It belongs with you."

Ethel hooked one hand around LeRoy's forearm; she slipped the other around his back. "It's beautiful," she said.

Sam undid the clasp and jumped off the coop. He ran to his parents and embraced them, a corner of the cover still clipped to his shirt collar. Ethel snapped away the cloth, grabbed it by two corners and twirled across the porch, the cloth billowing overhead. "Sure as the moon's gonna rise, there'll be music tonight."

LeRoy resisted. "I can't accept this." Gently he set the guitar down, leaning it against the railing.

The dance came to an end.

"Thank you, Hannah," LeRoy added.

Astonished, Hannah asked, "Why? Why not?"

"I just can't"

"I don't understand."

"I'm not a man who likes to carry debt."

Hannah shook her head in understanding, "No one does."

"I'm sorry."

"Is it because I'm white?"

The question caught LeRoy unawares. He spun around, stunned. He starred at Hannah, who refused to look away. After a long, awkward silence, LeRoy slowly turned and strolled to the end of the porch, looking off.

Sam remained still, glancing from parent to parent.

It was Ethel who made the next move. She walked up to Hannah and took hold of her, in the same way she had just held her husband. "Please understand. My husband is a proud man who has seen some terrible troubles. But thank you for the offer."

LeRoy turned. From the far end of the porch he said, "I accept. I accept your gift."

Sam squared off with Darla. "Who are you?"

"Her name's Darla," said Hannah.

"Do you want to go crawfish hunting?" he asked.

"Not now, honey." Ethel said, her eyes on LeRoy. "I'm making dumplings tonight. Would you and Darla like to join us?"

Hannah looked at LeRoy.

"Nobody makes a better dumpling than Ethel!" he said.

A relieved Ethel hugged herself. "Maybe, we'll get to hear LeRoy play a song or two. If he's willing."

That evening Hannah and Darla returned to the Williams' farm. Before dinner, Darla presented them with a drawing of Sam having his hair cut, drawn that afternoon from memory. After dinner, the group retired to the porch where LeRoy tuned the guitar. Sam straddled the railing, hugging his knees to his chest. After Ethel lit and placed around a series of candles to ward off mosquitoes, she and Hannah shared a pair of rocking chairs; Darla sat cross-legged on the bench, playing with the hem of her dress.

LeRoy began with *You Are My Sunshine.*

Nathan, the hotel proprietor and auctioneer, had a rich baritone voice. LeRoy had a seasoned, deep-earth bass, trapped underground, waiting for an earthquake to release its power. Hannah imagined the pair singing a duet.

He ended the second verse and motioned for Darla to come sit by him. After Darla had settled next to him, LeRoy took her hand and placed it on the belly of the guitar, above the row of strings. He began the third verse, watching Darla, waiting for her response.

It began with a small nod of the head. She flattened the palm of her hand even more. Then, slowly, a rocking side to side. Before long, her free hand began to register the rhythm of her and LeRoy's heartbeats.

*****

*****

Word of Darla's talent spread. Requests for portraits became more frequent.

Naomi asked to have Hannah and Darla meet her at the Creekside Mennonite Retreat Center by Cottonwood Lake.

When Hannah entered the center, Naomi had already created a setting for her portrait. There was a framed print of Paris, a wicker chair, a floor lamp with a glass-beaded fringe, and a side table brimming with a box of chocolates, grapes, cheese and a coke bottle sporting a homemade label, *Wine*.

Naomi was unrecognizable.

"*Bonjour*," she said, greeting her guests as she removed her glasses and held them upright.

"What have you been reading?" Hannah asked, eyeing the getup.

Delicately she rested her glasses on the table top. "*Chéri. The Ladies' Paradise. The Razor's Edge.*"

She wore a dress so outrageous it would not have been seen anywhere in Kalb County other than at a costume party. Naomi eased into the chair, hanging a leg over the side while draping an arm over her head. Unfolding her other arm, Naomi hooked her forefinger over her lower lip.

"What do you think, Darla?"

"Darla needs to be able to see your lips when you talk if you want her to understand you," Hannah instructed.

"*Quel étourdi. Excusez-moi.*"

"Nor does she know French."

Naomi responded by speaking loudly, over-enunciating, moving her mouth in an exaggerated, almost grotesque, fashion. "Do. You. Like. My. Pose?"

Darla nodded and pretended to brush dust off her sketch pad. Hannah took a seat next to the wall.

For a few minutes, Darla sketched in silence.

"Hannah, I want you to know I always disagreed with Eli's decision." Naomi said.

"Did you tell him that?" asked Hannah.

"No."

"Well, the time to speak up was then. It does no good telling me now."

Naomi tried not to take offense. "Will your anger with Eli always include me?"

"You're his wife. Had you spoken up, he may have listened to you."

"Oh? You never held your tongue against your husband to keep the peace?"

"Yes, I did. Often."

"Then don't pretend to be holier than me."

Her comment may have sounded like an accusation, but it wasn't hurled in malice or spite. Her eyes were filled with sadness. Tears were making their way down her cheeks.

Hannah refused to soften.

"Does Eli know you're here?"

"No."

"Has he seen your costume?"

"No."

"Have you talked to him about the books you've been reading?"

"No."

"And why is that?"

"Can't I have a life separate from his?"

"Yes. Yes, you can. If that's what you want."

"You want me to confront him? To fly off to Paris? Turn my back on God? Is that what you're suggesting?"

"I don't know what I'm suggesting," replied Hannah. "Honestly, I don't."

Both retreated into themselves.

For twenty minutes no one spoke.

"Look Homeward, Angel" Naomi whispered.

"What?"

"Look Homeward, Angel."

"What about it?"

"Laura falls in love with Eugene. But she's engaged; she has a fiancée in Richmond. In the end, Laura chooses her fiancée." Naomi closed her eyes. "Every time I read the book, I keep hoping Laura chooses Eugene."

"You want to rewrite Mr. Wolfe's book?"

"Yes. Yes, I do. I want to drink a Black Rose in *Café de la Rotonde*. I want to rewrite Eli's sermons. I want to read somewhere in the *New Testament* that Jesus dances. I want to hear God swear." She paused. "But I can't. I can't."

Hannah gazed at Naomi and said, "That's a pretty dress."

*****

*****

Wanda recommended a doctor known for performing abortions. She called the office and made an appointment for one week later.

"Rather than drive back to Adele after seeing the doctor, why don't you spend the night here," Wanda encouraged Hannah. "The procedure can be a knockout. Rest will do a world of good for your friend. I know."

"I should get back for my Thursday Calico route. I do have a bed in the Metro," Hannah replied.

"Calico?"

"It's a stream. The road follows it for a good part of my route," Hannah said, sorting through the books Wanda had collected for her. She remembered that over a year ago she had pledged to visit Vivian, the Ruston County librarian. It still hadn't happened.

The following Wednesday Laverne accompanied Hannah to St. Louis. Driving south, deeper into the broad, flat Mississippi River Valley, Hannah contemplated how far she had strayed from the teachings of her church. Folks at Creekside would have insisted that Laverne have the child. She glanced in the mirror. Would a time come when she stopped wearing her head covering?

Five Paws made it his mission to calm the anxious Laverne. He perched on her lap, planted his front paws on Laverne's chest and dappled her face with small, crescent kisses.

"What did you tell Frank and Norma?" asked Hannah.

"I said my friend Lizzie wanted me to go shopping with her for bridesmaid's dresses. I feel bad about lying."

They passed a string of tractor trailer trucks filled with livestock.

"What would you have told them?"

After a moment, Hannah replied, "My friend Wanda is moving to Arizona to become a pilot. I want to see her off."

"That doesn't sound like a lie."

"Ask me in a year."

On the return trip, Laverne flipped through a *Glamour* magazine from the doctor's waiting room: *10 funny ways to find a man on a beach* by Gloria Steinem. Laverne alternated between reading the article and bursting into tears. "I should be reading the Bible," she confessed.

*****

*****

On Saturday, Hannah followed through on her promise. She headed to Willmar where she planned a stop at the General Store before dropping by the library. Darla, free of school duties, relished the excursion. Last time Hannah visited the store, she recalled that Hugo Blackwell carried an impressive collection of art supplies. Darla brought a change purse filled with bills and coins – money she had collected from sales of her portraits.

When they entered the store Mr. Blackwell was lecturing a policeman who held a young boy by the scruff of his neck.

"... *If thy hand offend thee, cut it off; it is better for thee to enter into life maimed than, having two hands, to go into hell, into the fire that never shall be quenched.*"

Hearing Hugo's recitation, Hannah assumed the child had been caught shoplifting.

"Mr. Blackwell," the policeman begged. "It was a pack of gum. I've offered to pay you twice the amount it costs. Out of my own pocket."

"And what lesson will the boy learn from that?"

"Charity," the officer said, without missing a beat.

"Charity!" sniffed Hugo, his face turning red.

"*Though I speak with the tongues of men and of angels and have not charity, I am become as sounding brass or a tinkling cymbal,*" quoted the policeman. He released the boy. "Let this be the last time, taking something that doesn't belong to you! Now go!"

Darla quickly found and began to study the assortment of paints and brushes.

Apparently, Hugo considered Darla another thief, in conspiracy with the pardoned boy. He was not about to remain defenseless behind the counter. He sidled up to Darla, pretending to fuss over the alignment of tubes in the display. "May I help you?"

Darla stared at him.

"Are you looking for a particular brand? Or color?"

Darla shook her head and signed: I. Don't. Speak.

Hugo backed up, as if the girl oozed a contagious disease. He scurried over to Hannah.

"Does she not comprehend what I'm saying?"

"Darla's deaf," Hannah said.

"Does it affect her mind?"

"Some folks are short on reason, Hugo," Hannah replied. "Darla's short on talk."

Hugo seemed confused. "I saw a boy once without arms."

"Because Darla can't hear, she doesn't talk," Hannah explained, "not in the usual way."

Hugo was unconvinced.

Hannah left him, her lips pursed. She felt her fingers clench, forming a vice-tight grip as she paced the aisles. Deciding to buy a game of checkers, she spent the remaining time waiting for Darla to select her paints and brushes. They met at the register, but Hannah slipped in front of Darla, placing the game box on the counter.

After paying, Hannah said, "Hugo, do you have a few minutes to spare? For a game of checkers?"

Hugo nodded and Hannah opened the box, dumping out the chips and unfolding the board. As Hugo began placing the white chips on his side, Hannah announced, "Hugo, I need to feed the parking meter." She gestured to Darla and added, "Darla, do you mind?"

Darla stepped in, set the black chips in order and made the first move. With a series of quick, deft moves, Darla captured all of Hugo's chips.

Hugo was not amused.

"Another," he proposed.

Darla held up her finger. She placed a tube of paint between them. Hugo understood. It was a challenge. Were she to win, the tube of paint was free.

Unnoticed, Hannah quietly slipped in the front door and waited behind a rack of homemade aprons.

The second game passed quicker than the first.

Not about to quit, Hugo gathered two paint tubes and put them up for gamble.

Although Hugo managed to maneuver a chip across the board and be crowned king, Darla stifled his glee by jumping and capturing three unprotected white chips in one move. The third game ended in a third loss for Hugo.

Darla gathered together the remaining tubes of paint. "All or nothing," she gestured.

Humiliated but determined, Hugo accepted.

The game lasted longer than the previous ones, but only because Darla allowed it. Hugo's final chip was blocked in a corner. Unable to move, he had to admit defeat just as Hannah stepped forward from behind the brightly ruffled aprons with their bold borders of rickrack.

*****

*****

It was clear to Hannah that Vivian didn't recognize her. Not wishing to embarrass her or explain the situation under which they met, Hannah decided to forego any mention of their meeting at the General Store two years ago.

Vivian wore a striped, buttoned vest and a scarf that really wanted to be a necktie. It was held in place with a sliver pin.

What stuck Hannah most was that Vivian seemed to instantly understand Darla's situation.

"I run a small retail business," Hannah explained, "and if the library discards books from time to time, I wonder if you might consider selling them to me?"

"Most books we take out of inventory are too damaged, frankly, to be worth much. But we are known to give away duplicates, especially when we host the annual community book fair."

"Well, I'm interested. Could I leave you my name and contact information?"

"Of course."

"And I'm also curious if you could show Darla any art books you have?"

"I'd be happy to assist you."

Vivian pushed her chair away from the desk and stood up. Her trousers, though darker in color, perfectly complemented her vest. She picked up several unmarked library cards and a pen.

Vivian led the way.

When they paused to preview the books, Hannah asked, "Do you have any favorite artists?"

"I do!" Vivian said enthusiastically, but with a note of caution. "Tell me. Do you have a favorite artist?"

"Growing up, I always liked Grant Wood. But maybe that's because his work is familiar to me."

"An interesting man. He studied in Paris but spent most of his life in Iowa."

"Iowa has a lot in common with Missouri," ventured Hannah.

"Yes. Yes, it does. I'm partial to Matisse, but I would most want to have dinner with Hannah Gluckstein."

"Hannah Gluckstein? I don't know her." Hannah admitted.

"British. Her portraits are unconventional, but stunning. Some of her subjects are delightfully ambiguous."

Vivian handed Darla a card and the pen. She passed a hand across the spine of several books then raised both hands and shoulders.

Darla wrote: *How to Paint. Famous Portraits. Deaf Artists.*

Only two books interested Darla.

Vivian nodded. "We are a small midwestern library, after all."

They walked to the end of the row of shelves.

"How did you become a librarian?"

Vivian looked at each of them. She had ascertained Darla read lips, but was unsure what to say.

"I was an unwanted child of a single mother. She treated the library like a kennel whenever she wanted the house to herself to entertain friends."

Hannah appreciated her bluntness.

"But it wasn't all grim. I met my best friend at the library." After a pause, she added, "*Former* best friend."

Hannah knew, given the weight of her words, Vivian implied something beyond best friends.

"Shall we try the reference section?"

In a two-volume guide, Hannah uncovered a list of deaf painters that included John Brewster Jr., Juan Navarrette, Sampson Towgood Roch and Benjamin Ferrers.

"I can't say I'm familiar with any of them. Let me see what I can find out about them and, if you like, I could send you the information."

Hannah wrote her address on the back of another card. Tired of playing letter carrier, Nathan had insisted Hannah get a box at the post office.

*****

*****

In mid-November, as Hannah was preparing to travel south, she found an envelope tucked under the Metro windshield. The note was from Velma Butler, requesting that Hannah stop by her woodworking shop. Hannah was familiar with the small shingled building, with its green shutters and three-armed chimney, but she had never been inside.

She knocked on the door and was greeted by a gangly but broad-hipped woman with a wide gap between her front teeth. Velma wore denim overalls but the clasps that held the shoulder straps in place had been replaced with two copper door knobs that looked surprisingly like a pair of polished breasts.

"Thank you for coming, Hannah. Welcome to the dustbin."

Hannah chuckled, enthralled at the smell of freshly worked wood.

"It used to belong to my grandfather, but he's gone. Dad happily turned the operation over to me." She ran her hand over the arm of a rocking chair that was resting on the work table. "Beer?"

"No, thank you."

She picked up a half-finished bottle from the side bench and took a swig. "I not only repair and restore furniture, I design and build from scratch."

Hannah wondered what Velma would make of her makeshift screwed-together furniture in the van.

Opening the potbelly stove, Velma threw a handful of scraps down its throat.

"So why did Velma invite Hannah to her wood shack, you're wondering."

"I am curious."

"Velma makes small cedar chests and was wondering if Hannah would consider taking a few on consignment and try selling them?"

Hannah scanned the shop.

From under the table, Velma pulled out a large box, covered by a dust cloth. Inside was a collection of velvet drawstring bags, each containing a hidden treasure. From one of the bags Velma slipped a small, hinged box, a pattern of playful swirls delicately carved in its top. In the center of the lid, Velma had inset a fanfare of semi-precious gems.

"It's beautiful!" exclaimed Hannah. "May I open it?"

"Please."

Given the depth of the carving, Hannah hadn't expected such thin walls. The un-trapped fragrance transported her to the world of her grandmother with her seasoned handkerchiefs. She placed the chest, with its graceful scalloped feet, back on the table.

"I'll see what I can do," promised Hannah.

*****

*****

The row of forsythia shrubs had still not unlocked their buds as Hannah turned into the Williams' driveway late in March 1964. Trying to avoid the fresh ruts in the gravel path, Hannah noticed in the meadow a pair of unfamiliar skeletal posts surrounded by a small patch of blackened earth. The truck thumped over the bridge and began its climb to the farm-house. The long trek south and back, Hannah noticed, had ruffled the normally unflappable Metro.

LeRoy was first out of the house, followed by Sam.

"Miss Hannah," Sam shouted! "We missed you!"

Hannah backed the truck around and slipped out. "What's going on down in that meadow of yours, LeRoy?"

"Some white folks' way of telling us we black folks aren't welcome around here."

Hannah placed her fists on her hips and did a slow twist of her head. "Was it a cross burning?"

"No. Nothing like that. More civilized."

By now Ethel had joined the group. "It was a right proper sign. Done up real well. Must've taken somebody a goodly time to build it."

"Oh, Lord," sighed Hannah.

"There were gunshots about three in the morning. LeRoy was the first to see the gang. From the bedroom window."

"Someone had stapled kerosene-soaked letters to chicken wire and hung it on those two posts."

"They were big letters. On fire. So tall we could read them from the house."

"GO HOME," LeRoy and Ethel said together.

"We tried to keep Sam from seeing…." Ethel said.

LeRoy placed his arm around his son.

"Does anybody have any idea who might do such a thing?" asked Hannah.

"We saw a truck drive off but nobody got caught. Thank-fully," he added, "we weren't in a dry spell. The fire burned itself out, before the fire department got here."

"Where's Darla?" Sam asked.

"She's still in school," explained Hannah. "You'll have to wait until summer to see her."

"Will we be here in the summer, Dad?"

"We're not going anywhere, honey," Ethel vowed, but the current of doubt was unmistakable.

"Papa wrote a song about the burning," Sam said.

"He did now?" replied Hannah.

"He's got my name in the song."

"Does he?"

"And mama's, too."

"You think you might want to give the song a hearing?" asked Hannah.

LeRoy rocked back on his heels. "You're joshing me."

"Nathan, who owns Adele Motor Lodge, has a weekly radio show *Kalb County Speaks*. And my friend Larry performs at *The Stockyards*. They might give you a 'come-on-down.'"

"No."

"It's worth an ask."

"No."

"You mind if I ask them?"

"Hannah, Hannah, Hannah," LeRoy said, slipping into song. "I got a family to think of."

"I'm not pressuring you."

"No offense, Hannah. White folk don't want to hear what black folks have to say."

"LeRoy, I listen to the radio in my Metro. And there's plenty of singers out there who are colored."

"Yeah, singing, *He's so Fine... Be My Baby....*"

"Just keep playing guitar and writing songs, LeRoy. Keep playing and singing."

*****

*****

Velma and Hannah sat on the stoop of the woodworking shed. Hannah was drinking sun tea that Velma had prepared earlier in the day. Velma was cleaning a set of clasps and hinges with a wire brush.

"Every time I pass your shop, morning or evening, the light is on, "Hannah said. "Don't you ever stop working?"

"I like to keep busy."

"Jig saws and varnish. Sandpaper and glue. Is there nothing else to occupy your time?"

"Are you trying to marry me off, Hannah?"

"I've been known to take an interest in people's romantic lives," Hannah cracked.

"Well, your interest won't get very far with me," Velma retorted.

Hannah shifted to ease the pain in her back. "Velma, have you heard anything about what happened at the Williams' Farm?"

"I know what happened. But more than that, no, nothing."

"It troubles me that we have such hateful people among us. Doesn't it trouble you?"

"Ever since the assassination there's been a change. Haven't you sensed it?"

"Yes, I do. I feel it. A change in mood."

"It's not good to listen to the news. It makes us grumpy," Velma concluded.

"They have a boy. Sam. I worry what the times are doing to him."

Simon and Gerald would be eleven and fourteen now, Hannah thought. She crossed her arms and with her fingertips slowly stroked her forearms.

"This past winter in Florida, one Sunday morning, I had an urge to make my way back into church. To sit in a pew next to a lady in a freshly pressed dress or a man with a starched shirt, wearing too much cologne. There were no Mennonite churches in the area where I was staying. But there were plenty of Baptist churches. 'Mennonites are anabaptists,' I said. They can't be all that different. I had no idea the church I selected was a black house of worship."

She leaned back, relishing the memory.

"I'd never felt so welcome in God's House as I did that morning. The music. The joy. The dancing. The poetry of it all." Her eyes were misty. "Horace, my deceased husband, had nothing to do with church. But he would have felt at home there. He would have felt at home."

Velma, who had stopped polishing the hardware, asked ever so gently, "What about you? Is Hannah romancing anyone?"

"I'm still married to Horace."

"Doesn't it get lonely? On the road? Without a home?"

"I'm lonely, mostly, when I'm in Florida, alone," Hannah said.

Velma leaned over and kissed Hannah on the cheek.

Hannah rephrased Velma's question, "Doesn't it get lonely here, in your grandfather's shadow?"

*****

*****

Mad Dewey Hansen, a closet alcoholic, and his wife, Thelma, owned and operated Dewey's Orchard. They were part of Hannah's Cottonwood Lake circuit. Whatever was fresh, whatever was in season, Hannah knew on her visits she'd be treated to a basket of free produce. Thelma was sweet as applesauce but had the look of a sour-as-persimmon crone: thin blue lips, thinning hair, a spattering of moles sprouting thin, blue hairs. Mad Dewey never failed to ask Hannah if she sold SenSen breath fresheners. Long ago, his neck had disappeared into his chin. Neither firm nor tucked, it had the wiggle of a turkey's wattle.

From the Dewey homestead, Hannah took a shortcut to Route 57, driving a service lane though the orchard. Halfway down the private lane was a field shop.

On this day Hannah noticed a collection of large letters leaning against the cinderblock wall of the shop. Nearby was a roll of chicken wire and several creosote-treated posts.

Hannah stopped the truck. Darla, who was attempting to tie a cherry stem into a knot with her tongue was catapulted into the dash. Hannah looked in her rear view mirror. She looked left and right, between the rows of plum trees, then got out. She went to investigate the scene and saw six oversize letters cut from plywood: I G N G R E.

Darla, with a fistful of cherries, joined her.

Hannah's first instinct was to throw the letters in the turnaround and drive over them, but as she kicked them with the toe of her shoe, another thought occurred to her. She would back her Metro into the posts, cracking them in half.

Convinced she'd rendered the posts useless, Hannah turned the Metro around and headed back to Dewey's house. A wide-eyed Darla didn't make a single gesture.

Hannah knocked desperately on the front door. Thelma raced to see who had summoned her, a rolling pin in hand.

"Where's Dewey," asked Hannah.

"I thought you left."

"I need to see Dewey."

"What's wrong?"

"Do you know where he's at?"

"Dewey!" Thelma screamed at the top of her lungs.

Dewey emerged from the packing shed, juiced and a bit waxed in the ankles. "What's all the commotion?"

Running to him, Hannah exclaimed, "I'm afraid I was a careless driver just now."

"Slow down. Do I need to call an ambulance?"

"No, no. I did a turn-around out by the orchard shop and accidentally bumped into some posts. It's my fault. I want to make it right."

"A turn-around? Did you forget something?" Thelma asked. "Were the cherries bad?"

"No...." Hannah stammered, searching for an answer. "I stopped to empty the chamber pot. In the orchard. Among the trees. I didn't think anybody would mind."

Dewey rolled his eyes.

"I don't think the posts are usable. The bumper splintered them up good. But I'll buy you a new set, Mr. Dewey. I'll bring them next time. In two weeks, when I return."

Dewey scratched his head. "Thank you, Hannah. But I was planning to use them before then."

"Oh?" Hannah exclaimed. "Well, I can run over to the lumber yard anytime and get them straightaway. When do you need them?"

"Sunday, next."

"Well, then I'll bring them by this weekend. Will that do?"

"That'll be fine. If I'm not here, put 'em next to the damaged ones. Thank you, Hannah. If you'd been one of my workers and smacked those posts, you never would'a said a word."

Driving Route 57, Hannah stared straight ahead, not saying a word. As they approached the next stop, she pulled over to the side of the road. She turned to Darla and motioned for her to get her sketch book. "Hand it to me," she indicated. Hannah found an empty page and wrote "Draw Mr. Dewey." She handed the sketch book back to Darla.

*****

*****

Frances had postponed celebrating Darla's birthday to a night when Hannah could join them for dinner. All had been banned from the kitchen and dining room. Despite Hannah's objections, Darla asked her father to look at the driver's window on the Metro. When turning the handle, it failed to fully engage. The window would drop in a series of jerks as the lever spun in its socket. Quincy removed the side door panel.

Adam rode up on his bike and bumped the front tire against the Metro.

"Stop it," Quincy begged.

Adam rode off, did a few loops in the driveway and returned, once again, to tap the tire several times against the truck.

"Adam! I'm trying to work!"

Quincy identified the trouble. The gear wasn't stripped. The bolt binding the lever had simply loosened. He tightened the fixture and reinstalled the panel.

It was a festive table, adorned with fresh flowers and scissor-blade-curled ribbons. "Do you like the chicken?" Frances asked her son.

Adam didn't respond.

"What do you think is in the package?" Quincy pantomimed, pointing to the wrapped box on the sideboard.

Darla gave her father a really-are-you-asking-me-that look. She plucked the shoulders of her blouse. It was a dress, surely, sewn by her mother.

Frances turned to Adam, "Would you like some more roasted potatoes?"

He didn't answer.

When they were through, Hannah cleared the plates. "Before dessert, I would like Darla to open her gift."

Darla unwrapped the brightly-colored paper to reveal a plain box determined not to announce its contents. She undid the tab, reached in and pulled out a camera.

"Thank you!" she gestured, clearly unprepared for what she held in her hands.

"Birthday cake!" Frances announced and disappeared into the kitchen. She returned — fourteen glowing candles on a rose-studded angel food cake – and placed the confection before Darla. "Happy birthday, sweetheart."

Darla lifted the cake and held it out to Adam, signaling that he should blow out the candles.

Adam shook his head.

"Adam, is something wrong?" asked Frances.

No response.

When Adam refused a piece of cake, Frances could no longer contain herself. "Adam! What's going on! You haven't said a word all evening."

"I'm deaf!" screamed Adam as he stood up. He picked up his plate and threw it hard onto the floor. It shattered, pieces exploding across the floor.

Quincy rose. "Adam!"

Adam grabbed the camera from the table and began circling the table, pretending to take pictures of everyone.

Horrified, Darla rose and ran from the dining room.

Quincy chased his son, caught him and was about to say something but remained speechless. He simply stared at a boy he didn't recognize. He grabbed the camera just as Adam was about to hurl it across the room.

Hannah met Frances in the kitchen. "I can't help feeling this is my fault, Frances."

Frances leaned against the counter, shaking her head in disbelief. She turned around, tears in her eyes. "I don't know who I should go to. Darla or Adam?"

Hannah found the broom. She walked into the dining room and began sweeping together the broken pieces.

*****

*****

Ethel embraced the idea wholeheartedly, much to Hannah's surprise. It was LeRoy who needed convincing. With their consent, Hannah made a phone call to Wanda, explaining the sign-burning incident and expressing her wishes.

"What's next?" Wanda asked, enraged. "Are they going to set fire to the farmhouse? Like those goons who bombed the Baptist Church in Birmingham, killing four little girls?"

After hanging up, Wanda called a former high-school classmate, Maddie Hornberger. The star shot putter was thrilled to round up a clutch of rugged women primed to create a ruckus.

Hannah met the gang in St. Louis, in the parking lot of *Cantor's Warehouse and Supply Center.*

Maddie had a severe underbite, making her chin look like the prow of a snowplow. Her wiry hair was twisted into two short, tight pigtails. Greta had the face of juggling balls frozen in midair: large, round, red cheeks and a matching large, round, red chin. Sissy had never recovered from her severe case of adolescent acne. Her dark hair was limp and straggly. Stacy seemed to be built from a series of blocks, angular and staunch as a cubist painting. Wanda was the designated driver.

Hannah introduced herself, then shared Darla's drawing of Mad Dewey. "He appears to be the ringleader," she said.

"I don't like him," chimed in Maddie.

"It's nearly a three-hour to Adele," continued Hannah.

"Not the way I drive," interrupted Wanda.

"You'll come up Sunday morning and we'll take a look around. Get ready. We might want to take naps because we'll be up all night. You'll drive back Monday."

"Naps? Who needs naps?"

"I want to be clear. I can't guarantee there'll be a second sign-burning. These guys may never show. It's only a hunch."

"Oh, it'll happen," predicted Stacy.

Wanda, impatient to speak, broke in, "Should we bring weapons?"

"I know how to shoot bow and arrows."

"My brother has a shotgun I can borrow."

"Where could we get some hand grenades?"

"I like the idea of torches."

"No, no, no," Hannah nearly shouted. "We don't want a war."

"What else is there?"

"If there isn't bloodshed, what's the point?"

"We want to scare them. Not hurt them."

"You gotta hurt somebody to scare them!" insisted Stacy.

"I don't want us breaking the law."

"What about these guys? Aren't they breaking the law?"

"Trespassing."

"Vandalism."

"Arson."

Hannah agreed. "Yes. They're breaking the law."

"Well, an eye for an eye."

"That's what the Bible says."

Hannah took a deep breath. "I can't have us breaking the law."

"I do it all the time," Greta smirked.

"If we break the law and get caught, what do you think happens?" asked Hannah. "Would a judge or jury take our side? Not in Kalb County."

"There are ways to untwist a judge," offered Sissy.

Hannah continued, "If we don't stop them, these thugs will likely keep on doing what they're doing. Maybe even pull in more people, sympathetic neighbors, to help their cause."

"God, what century do your neighbors live in?" asked Maddie.

"Why us?" Sissy asked, cracking her knuckles.

"You're not from the area," explained Hannah. "Nobody will recognize your faces or voices." She passed the drawing of Dewey around a second time. "It's important we let Dewey know we know his name. His wife's name. That he likes Old Crow whiskey. That he drives a blue '61 Buick Riviera."

"You guys all heard of Percy Green, right?"

"Yeah!"

"Who's he?"

"The dude who infiltrated the construction site at the Gateway Arch and climbed partway up one of the legs," explained Maddie.

"Yeah," continued Wanda, "He and his buddy, this white guy named Daly, locked themselves to the ladder."

"Why'd they do that?"

"It was their way of protesting the contractors, who refused to hire black workers."

Sissy, charged up, was milking the strings of her hair. "They hung out for five hours before they were finally talked down."

Stacy announced, "A friend of a friend knows Percy. She says Percy and his buddy are, like, these righteous rebels ... with a cause."

"Well, this is our Percy moment," vowed Maddie.

"What should we wear?" asked Sissy.

Hannah bit her lip. "I'm still working on that."

*****

*****

When Hannah pulled on the Ruston County Library door handle, she discovered it was locked. She looked around the alcove for a sign posting the hours of operation. Vivian, seated inside behind her desk, noticed Hannah and scrambled to the front door to unlock it.

"Hannah, come in!" Locking the door behind her, Vivian rested her hand on Hannah's shoulder and said, "Nice to see you."

Hannah took her hand and looked into her eyes. "Is everything okay?"

"Yes. I just came in early to do some research. And you? What are you up to?"

"Where would I find records on local residents?"

"What are you looking for?"

"Anything, really. Titles. Deeds. Convictions. Court rulings."

"Let me show you. There's quite a bit to sort through."

Thirty minutes later Hannah approached Vivian, who closed the book she was reading and pushed it, along with another book, under a low shelf.

"Where would I find books on Genealogy?"

"Salt Lake City," Vivian joked. "No, really, we have quite a few family tree books here."

Hannah lingered over the books, waiting patiently for Vivian to be distracted. When Vivian went to the bathroom, Hannah stepped behind the desk to inspect the books she had been reading: *A Guide to Cancer. Chemotherapy or Radiation?*

Hannah retreated to a far corner of the library and sat on a loose-jointed oak chair.

She had intended to peruse books on ghosts, phantoms and scourges.

But they had come to her.

She finished her investigations by checking *The Farmer's Almanac*. Slowly she made her way back to Vivian's desk.

"I know someone who could do a marvelous job restoring your chairs," she said.

*****

*****

The energy of the girls was hard to contain. After exploring the farm, selecting hideouts, setting traps and chowing down on Ethel's slow-cooked ribs and grits, they were fit to be tied.

They congregated in an unused bedroom on the second floor.

Each warrior began decorating her face with Darla's paints, infused with Tide laundry detergent so the designs would glow in the dark.

LeRoy sat, legs spread, elbows on his knees, watching the girls. "One look at you gals and those gun-slinging fools will head to the hills."

"Guns?!" exclaimed Greta.

"You never said they had guns!" cried Sissy.

"They only fired them to wake us up," Ethel explained.

"Oh, I guess they're just noise makers. No need to worry about bullets."

"Hannah, what have you thrown us into?" asked Greta in an accusatory manner.

"Girls!" Maddie barked. "I got you covered."

Wanda shifted uneasily in her chair.

"I brought the hand grenades," Maddie announced, casting a sideways glance at Hannah. The other warriors stopped applying makeup and turned to Hannah.

"That's a joke, right?" Hannah demanded.

"Maybe it is. Maybe it isn't."

"Maddie," Hannah warned, "if you have any intention of using grenades, I'll call the whole thing off."

"Come on now, Miss Hannah," Maddie replied. "Don't you know a joke when you hear one?"

Hannah remained unconvinced.

"What if they don't park on the road like last time," LeRoy said, "but drive down the lane, instead?"

"Stop fretting," shushed Maddie.

"What if they park on the bridge?"

"We're screwed."

"Stop being such a piker," Maddie countered, irritated at any trace of apprehension.

"Whatever they do," Hannah said, "I hope Dewey doesn't hang by the truck and have his buddies do the work of digging holes and hanging the sign. That would be like him."

Just the mention of Dewey's name brought Maddie back into the game. She had a different take on Dewey. "Nah. He'll lead the way. He'll be the one to light the sign."

Earlier the girls had memorized obscure, incriminating tidbits about Dewey, dug up by Hannah at the Ruston County Public Library. Naming his transgressions would hopefully spook the orchard grower.

While the sun set, the St. Louis gang began to slip into their costumes: hooded cloaks with rubber snakes, newts and miniature plastic skulls sewn to them – all prepared in secret by Frances. They distributed noise makers and instruments of torture. Hannah moved the van into the barn.

At dusk all lights were turned off and the ladies departed the house, walking down the lane or cutting across the lawn, each heading toward her post. Hannah, LeRoy, Ethel and Sam climbed out a bedroom window and sat on the roof of the porch.

"Not much of a moon tonight," LeRoy said, "just as Hannah predicted."

"It were no prediction," Ethel replied.

One might have thought Hannah had training in tactical arts as the girls rigorously headed to their stations.

Maddie and Stacy, the most muscular of the lot, slipped under the bridge. Sissy climbed the expansive maple tree next to the bridge, its roots forming an embankment along the water. She tucked a blanket into the crotch of two branches and settled into her perch. Testing the pair of ropes rigged that afternoon, Sissy determined the system was in perfect working order. Wanda crouched behind the water trough at the top edge of the meadow. Greta nestled next to the garden fence, between rows of sunflowers, and covered herself with branches.

As night deepened, fewer and fewer cars passed the Williams' farm. Just after midnight, Greta returned to the farmhouse. Hannah and Ethel squeezed back in through the window and hurried down the stairs.

"What's going on?"

"Is anything wrong?"

"Do you have a flashlight?" asked Greta.

"Yes. Why?"

Greta looked at the floor. "I was playing with my ring and lost it in the dirt."

"We'll look for it in the morning," Hannah promised.

"Why were you playing with your ring?" Ethel asked.

"I dunno." Greta replied.

"It's okay," Ethel assured Greta, "We'll find it tomorrow. Promise. We're all a little nervous."

Around two in the morning a pair of headlights could be seen far ahead as a vehicle slowly made its way down the road. About to crest a low hill, the lights were turned off.

"This is them," whispered LeRoy.

The engine was cut and the vehicle coasted to a stop at the end of the Williams' lane. Two men jumped from the bed of the truck and two emerged from the cab. Without a sound, they lifted the sign and walked it backwards, over the edge of the tailgate. Someone hiked the posts over his shoulder; another reached into the bed of the truck and pulled out two rifles, a shovel and fuel container. The group began their trek down the Williams' lane, bordered on each side by a fence.

They crossed over the bridge. There were approximately fifty more yards to travel before reaching the gate leading to the pasture.

Soon after the footsteps overhead passed, Maddie and

Stacy emerged from each side of the bridge. They lifted a wide plank and moved it forward one foot, directly in front of the gap. Sissy pulled on the ropes. From beneath the bridge a crossbar, to which a net was attached, was hoisted up. She loosely tied the ropes to a thick, overhead branch. Noiselessly Sissy shimmed down the tree. She raced along the wheat field, jumping the fence by the road in a single bound. Deftly, she pulled the latch to the hood, raising it a few inches. Without fumbling, Sissy grabbed a fistful of spark plug wires and yanked them free, tossing them by the side of the road, then returned to her perch in the shelter of the maple tree.

Greta removed the branches covering herself and took a few low steps along the fence, toward the lane, where she grabbed a braided rope to which a dozen empty tin cans had been attached.

Wanda gripped the striking cap.

Just as the men were undoing the latch on the gate. Wanda sparked the emergency road flare and began blowing shrilly on her whistle. Throwing the striking cap aside, she held the flare high overhead. With her free hand, she picked up a kettle filled with rocks. A crazed Wanda began racing down the lane toward the intruders.

From the opposite side of the lane, Greta began blasting a marine air horn. With the bundle of clanking tin cans trailing behind her, Greta joined Wanda. Together they charged.

The men dropped everything: sign, posts, shovel, rifles, metal fuel can. Wild-eyed and spooked, they started racing back down the lane toward their getaway truck.

When the frontrunners reached the bridge, they tripped over the repositioned plank. Any attempt to break their fall failed. Hands and feet slipped through gap and the men were sent sailing into the net, which fell down over them. It was a medical melee of twisted ankles, jammed wrists, scraped shins and crushed testicles.

The slowest member of the troop, also the heaviest, tumbled onto the bundle of compatriots trapped inside the net. His impact pushed the men further into the gap, creating a mass of wedged limbs and torsos.

The cowering men, surrounded by furies from hell, had still not comprehended the situation.

"Well, if it isn't Dewey Donovan," announced Maddie

"Hi, Dewey," the girls said in eerie unison.

The men looked up into the faces of their captors, illuminated by the faint red glow of the flare burning in the ditch. Jagged lines of white paint. Chevrons on cheeks. Dots. Slashes. Flashing eyes hidden in deep black hollows.

In their frazzled, euphoric state the girls failed to barrage Dewey with any of the incriminating facts they had memorized earlier about him.

Maddie pulled a smuggled pistol from her jeans and fired it into the air. She leaned over Dewey and grabbed him by the throat. "You ever set foot on this land again, a thousand dancing witches are gonna come outta the hills. They're gonna come up from the ground, crawling out of gopher holes, sniffing their way through your orchard, crawling up to your house. They're gonna walk through your walls, dance around your bed and sink their teeth into your manhood!"

Wanda added, "That goes for all of you!"

"Now, git!" added Maddie, releasing Mad Dewey.

The girls flipped back the net and watched the dumbstruck men struggle to their feet. One by one, as they freed themselves, they raced down the lane, toward the truck.

As the last man was approaching the truck, Maddie hurled her farewell.

The grenade exploded with a brilliant flash of light and geyser of dirt as the four men took refuge in a truck that held one final insult.

"Oh, hell." Hannah exclaimed on the porch roof.

The following morning Hannah and LeRoy gathered up the supplies left behind by the gang; Hannah noticed the can containing the fuel was misspelled *KEROCENE*.

*****

*****

Before her departure from Missouri that season, Hannah paid Vivian a visit. It was no accident that Hannah arrived fifteen minutes before closing.

"What are you researching today?" Vivian asked.

"Nothing found in any library book," replied Hannah, studying Vivian for any signs of ill health.

"How is your daughter?"

"Oh, Darla's not my daughter. But I consider her family nonetheless."

"She sent me a very nice note for the information I mailed to her."

"Not only is she gifted; Darla has a talent for perceiving things that escape most of us."

"I sensed that." Vivian shifted several piles of envelopes and invoices.

Adopting a playful tone, Hannah asked, "Have you arranged dinner with Hannah?"

Vivian gave Hannah a quizzical look.

"Your friend, the artist. I can't remember her last name."

"Oh! Hannah Gluckstein."

"Yes. Hannah Gluckstein."

"That would be rather difficult," Vivian admitted. "She lives in England and, I suspect, is nearly seventy years old."

Hannah ran her hand along the edge of the counter. "You don't remember the first time we met. I had just lost my husband and two boys. You offered books that might help me make sense of my situation...."

"Oh," Vivian said, shaking her head, "the general store?"

"Yes."

"Mr. Blackwell," Vivian confessed, "He can't keep anything to himself." She was about to continue, but decided against it.

"I suspect you need to make your closing rounds," volunteered Hannah.

"Come with me."

Vivian circled the library, pulling down blinds, turning off floor lamps and picking up pieces of discarded trash.

Hannah accompanied her. "Would you like to grab a coke at Walgreens?"

"That would be lovely; a coke sounds good, "Vivian admitted, "but I have an appointment."

Silently, Hannah considered the possibilities. A doctor's appointment? A visit to the pharmacist? Consulting a medical specialist?

Vivian saw her curiosity. "I'm to meet a lawyer. To sign papers."

It was impossible to discern much from Vivian's expression other than it was a troubling engagement.

"Next time. And not just a coke. Burgers and fries!" promised Vivian.

Hannah would leave baffled, with more questions unanswered than when she arrived. On the way out, she paused by the door and turned back. "I know someone who could do a marvelous job restoring your chairs," she said.

*****

*****

Saturday evening in early April 1965, Hannah put Five Paws in a basket and tied the lid shut. She slipped into an overcoat, pulling it over her head like a hood. Against the driving rain, she ran to the hotel lobby and knocked on the door. Nathan, stacking towels in the closet, came dashing to assist her.

"It's not locked! Just let yourself in!"

"That seems a bit blunt," Hannah said, "barging in unannounced."

"How many times have we sat in the lobby, like two old ladies gossiping and yelling at the TV? You don't need an invitation."

"You're a polite man. You like things proper."

Five Paws meowed.

Hannah placed the basket on a nearby chair. "I don't know what's bothering him. Normally rain on the roof doesn't spook him. Tonight, he's fit to be tied. Is something going on?" she asked, looking nervously around.

Nathan turned on the television. It was the *Jackie Gleason Show*. It would be followed on another channel by the *Lawrence Welk Show*. Nothing out of the ordinary.

Hannah picked up the basket, set it on the floor and sat.

"I've been thinking. It might be time to rent a room. Or one of your cottages," Hannah said. She paused to consider aloud, "How long has the truck been my home, now?"

"Would you like to spend tonight in a room? I can give you one if you like," offered Nathan, unaccustomed to seeing Hannah in such an agitated state.

"If you don't mind, I'd rather stay here. It's familiar. This chair practically doubles as a bed."

She placed the basket on her lap and slipped a finger under the lid. "Did you ever have a pet?"

"Our family had a Dalmatian. Oscar. I've only seen my father cry once. When he buried Oscar."

"What did he do? Your father?"

"You don't know?"

"Well, if I heard, I've forgotten."

"He was an undertaker."

"All that death," Hannah whispered, "and the only thing that troubles him is a dog."

Nathan shrugged.

"But he loved you. I hope he loved you."

"Yes. There was never any doubt."

"Oh, that's good!"

Nathan settled on the sofa next to Hannah.

"And your mother?"

"Now it gets complicated."

"It's hardly ever straightforward, is it?"

"She was always so concerned about our health. The moment we coughed, off to the doctor. The slightest fever, a visit to Doctor Larson. I suppose we learned, somehow, our being ill pleased her. It was only later, when I was older, I realized why."

"Your mother was in love with Doctor Larson?"

"Yes."

"That must have been dreadful," Hannah said. "But you're fine now."

Nathan chuckled goodheartedly. "I run a silly hotel. I have a little radio show no one listens to. I sell people's most treasured possessions and collect a shameful commission. I'm fine."

"Lord, listen to that wind," Hannah said.

"There's no need to keep Five Paws locked in his basket." Nathan said.

*****

*****

The following afternoon, Nathan knocked on the door to Hannah's van. "Have you heard?"

"What?"

"There were a whole band of tornadoes, from Iowa to Ohio. Over two hundred people killed. More than one hundred alone in Indiana."

"Five Paws, did you hear that? You had every reason to be spooked."

*****

*****

"Have you been to the Ruston County Public Library?" Hannah asked Velma.

"No. Should Velma have been to the Ruston County Public Library?" Velma asked with a tone of rebounding accusation.

"It's a handsome building," Hannah stated, "inspired by the Carnegie model. I especially like the interior." She took a sip of beer, having come to appreciate Velma's taste in beverages.

"Are the file drawers made with dovetail joints?"

"They are," Hannah admitted. "Because of you, I now notice these things."

"Are the label holders brass or tin?"

"Pewter."

"Very New England. The librarian? *Per*snickety or per*snick*ety?"

"Neither. We're quite friendly."

Velma applied a new, fine-grit paper to her sanding pad.

"I doubt you'd like her, though," lied Hannah.

"Oh? Why is that?"

"Not that you wouldn't admire her. I couldn't see her wearing one of your overalls, although she does favor more masculine clothes."

"What does that mean?"

"Let's not fight. We both know we're not hair-curler gals with manicured nails."

"In my line of work manicures would be pointless," Velma said, holding up her stained hands.

"Exactly."

"That doesn't mean I don't appreciate a nail that's been filed and polished."

Hannah smiled. "Despite the allure of the library, some of the furnishings are a bit fatigued."

"They need Velma's touch. Restoring them to their former glory? Is that where Hannah is going?"

"No. I want to start from scratch."

Velma sensed a change come over Hannah.

"Would you be willing to design and build three chairs?"

Velma put down her tools. "What do you have in mind?"

"They would be dedicated to my husband and sons. And they would live in the library."

"You've spoken to the librarian?"

"Her name is Vivian. Yes."

"She's agreeable?"

"Yes."

"I ask that you include their names. I don't know how. A plaque. A carving of some sort. That's up to you."

"Of course, Hannah. You know I'll do it. I hope you didn't doubt it for a second."

Hannah, misty-eyed, nodded gratefully. "Vivian and I agree. It would be nice if the design complemented the room in some way."

"A similar style. I get it," Velma said.

"I suppose that means we should plan a visit, so the three of us can meet."

Velma nodded in agreement.

"Vivian suggested a Sunday morning, when the library is closed."

*****

*****

Naomi's homemade banana ice cream cannot be resisted.

The invitation was delivered to Hannah's post office box. The note explicitly stated Eli would be out of town. Could Darla attend, as well?

Hannah stopped at a pay phone to telephone Naomi.

"You know how to reel in a fish," Hannah said into the receiver. "I'll be there."

The ice cream was served immediately, with Nabisco Vanilla Wafers. Clearly Naomi had an agenda. Sweets were the pretext.

Naomi was the first to empty her bowl. She stood up. "If you're wondering, Eli is in Cincinnati. Some religious book fair. He and the organist want to buy new hymnals." She winked at Hannah, "Communion is this Sunday. It might be a good idea to attend if you wish to remain in good standing."

"Is someone keeping track?"

"That's one of the jobs of a deacon," Naomi said, then disappeared into an adjoining room.

Darla picked up a second wafer. Casting a warning glance at Hannah, she snapped it in half.

Naomi returned with a stash of dresses still on their hangers, folded over her arm. She did her best to illustrate her words with a series of clumsy gestures.

"I've been going through my wardrobe. Darla, we're about the same size. If you're interested, I'd be happy to give them to you."

"That's very considerate," Hannah said.

"I decided they're just too plain for me."

Hannah took a quick breath. Why wouldn't Darla come to the same conclusion? Or was she more suited to plain?

"They're store-bought," Naomi added.

The comment riled Hannah even more. Even if they didn't reflect the latest fashion, the dresses sewn by Frances were far better crafted than anything one could buy in a department store.

Darla, however, was so entranced by the offer, Hannah decided to forego any response.

"Help yourself," Naomi said, throwing the garments over the back of a chair. "You can try them on in the next room." She picked up a small carton and sat next to Hannah.

"I was hoping you could help me dye my hair."

Hannah resisted a chuckle. "I've never dyed anyone's hair."

"Nor have I."

"You'd do better, I think, to visit a salon."

"It seems simple enough."

Hannah picked up the kit and turned it over. "Why?"

"Oh, Hannah! That's not the question! Why not?!"

"Your hair is already brown."

"I want to start subtle. Just a shade darker. Nothing so drastic so as Eli will notice." She laughed, "Blonde comes later."

Hannah opened the box. It contained a pair of disposable gloves, a bottle of dye and a conditioner to set the color.

"I wet my hair first, I believe," Naomi said. "We'll use the kitchen sink."

"How long do you leave it in?"

"It's like shampoo. Just until it takes. Oh, this'll be fun! We'll pretend we're girls, playing with dolls."

Hannah was having a hard time reading the fine print on the bottle. "It won't burn your scalp?"

Naomi grabbed the bottle from Hannah and peered at the directions. "Just a minute." She found her purse and fished out her glasses. When she put them on, Hannah noticed one lens was missing. "Fifteen minutes. It says fifteen minutes." She laid her glasses on the table, next to the plate of wafers.

Darla, who witnessed the exchange, wrote something on a notecard. When Naomi went to the kitchen to fill the sink,

Darla handed the note to Hannah. It read "Husband."

Hannah looked at Darla, signaling for an explanation. Darla pointed to the glasses and pretended to punch herself in the eye.

Other than staining a towel which Naomi discarded, the operation went smoothly.

They returned to the living room where Naomi repositioned a large Olympic fan to speed up the drying process.

"Next time, we'll dye your hair, Hannah." She paused from brushing her hair and looked around. "Gosh, it's nice having the place to myself."

Darla pointed out her selection to Naomi: two dresses with similar cuts, both in shades of blue.

"That's all?"

Darla nodded her head and signed, "Thank you."

"Now that I'm all done up," Naomi said, "we have to go out."

Hannah looked around for her purse and picked up the last of the wafers. "I should be taking Darla home."

"We can't have expended all that effort without inviting some small measure of appreciation! That would be a waste. Pure and simple."

"What do you have in mind?"

"My thought was for us to take Darla home and then go to *The Stockyards*."

Hannah couldn't contain her surprise. "You've been to *The Stockyards* before?"

"Did I dye my hair before?" Naomi asked, glancing at Hannah coyly. "Oh, I see what you're thinking. What's a deacon's wife doing in a bar?"

"That is not at all what I'm thinking. But you should expect others to think that."

Naomi wasn't the least bit nervous.

Acting like a regular, she walked up to Sonny, the bartender. "A black rose, please."

"A black what?"

"Rose. A black rose."

"Is that a drink or a freak of nature?" asked Sonny.

Naomi graciously excused Sonny. "Never mind. Just fix me something pretty and nice and sweet and cold. Your choice."

"That would be a beer," Sonny said.

Hannah noticed Larry at the far end of the bar, bent over a sheet of paper, a drink by his side. She slipped onto the chair next to him. "Let me guess. Writing a song?"

"More like…" Larry stalled, "it's writing me."

"That sounds frightening, but it sounds fitting."

"I guess, what I'm saying is… the song was there all along. When you get out of the way, it just shows itself."

Naomi claimed the chair on the opposite side of Larry. She turned to him and said, "Hello, handsome."

*****

*****

It was a joyful Sunday morning drive to Willmar. More than the usual number of blackbirds feasting in the meadows. The discovery of a herd of goats on the Webster farm. Country churches framed with polished cars and field-hardened pick-ups engaged in their own brand of worship.

Velma held a pinwheel she'd fashioned from thinly-planed veneers of maplewood. It spun enthusiastically in the wind. Darla, moving her lips ever-so-slightly, appeared to be singing. Was she thinking of LeRoy, Hannah wondered?

They were greeted by Vivian at the front door, who seemed a polished version of Velma. Denim and silk. Slacks and over-alls. Rawhide boots and scuffless leather pumps.

Darla immediately headed to the art book section.

Guided by Vivian, Hannah and Velma were shown about the library. As on her previous visit, Hannah studied Vivian for any signs of illness.

"I especially like the lamp fixtures. They have an art deco quality," Vivian said.

Velma nodded in agreement.

"See, here, on the floor? The filled-in screw holes? They once held flanges for a railing where people lined up at the circulation desk."

Velma paused to study the deep-set paneling encasing the open staircase to the second floor. She ran her fingers lightly over the molding, then stepped back to survey it from a distance. Moving to her left, Velma studied the design from an angle. Then she shifted to the right to get another view. Slowly, she moved her index finger along the underside of a raised frame until she felt a shallow recess. She paused, as if listening for a cue. Applying the smallest amount of pressure, the panel opened inward.

Vivian gasped.

They looked at one another in astonishment and awe.

"How did you? I never knew that was there!" exclaimed Vivian.

"Shall we explore?" asked Velma. She stepped inside the opening, then turned back.

"A flashlight," Vivian said, reading her mind.

For all its mystery, the enclosure seemed to only house a few paper-filled boxes.

"Something to explore in the future," Velma said.

When Hannah sensed Velma had satisfied her curiosity, she proposed they all go on a picnic to Cottonwood Lake. "Nathan gave me his word: it would be a gorgeous day, so I prepared a basket of sandwiches, chips and Dewey Orchard apples."

Vivian was visibly disappointed. "I'm afraid I have to stay here and attend to my mother."

"Your mother?" Hannah uttered.

"She has an aggressive form of ovarian cancer."

"I'm sorry," said Velma.

"It's ironic. She never really had time for me. And, yet, now that she's dying, who does she turn to? When she asked to move in with me, I couldn't say no. I'm her only child."

Velma placed her hand on Vivian's shoulder. "Is she able to walk?"

"A bit," Vivian replied. "She's pretty much confined to her bed... or a wheelchair."

"Why don't you bring her?"

"We have room," Hannah said.

"She can have my sandwich," added Velma.

Vivian shared looks with Hannah and Velma. "It's worth a try, I suppose."

Nattie turned out to be the life of the party. She laughed loudest of the lot and insisted Darla push her – wheelchair and all – into waist-deep water where she flapped her arms like a duck, splashing everyone.

Later, on the shore, Darla handed Hannah a note: "*I think Vivian likes Velma. Does Velma like Vivian?*"

A moment later Velma snuck up behind Hannah and snatched the note from her.

Velma sat down on the shore next to Darla and requested her pencil. She wrote something on the note and handed it back to Darla. *"She does."*

*****

*****

Quincy and Frances Leichty made a decision in May 1966 as the school year drew to a close. That summer Darla would not be traveling with Hannah. There would still be the bi-weekly suppers, but in deference to their son Adam, who continued his tantrums, Darla's time with Hannah would be limited.

Like other boys his age, Adam was swept up in the *Batman* frenzy. Many dinner conversations included a mention of the Joker, Robin or the Riddler.

A week prior to the movie's opening, Hannah posed a question. "Would you like me to arrange a showing for you and a friend?"

The boy's opinion of Hannah changed instantly. "Could you! Yes. Can I, Mom? Yes! Yes!"

"Who would you bring?"

"Pete. He owns every Batman toy there is. He has a utility belt and a Bat-Bomb. And a trace-a-graph!"

"I'll see what I can do," replied Hannah.

When Darla caught her mother's eye, signaling her desire to join the outing, Frances discreetly shook her head no.

The Ruston theater, seating a meager seventy patrons, was run by Otis Patron. Hannah explained her vision of the evening's itinerary and for a handsome fee, Otis promised to deliver.

Adam was delirious. None of his friends would have already seen the movie. Envied and revered, he would be their informer and guide. To add to the excitement, the movie would begin at a time when, normally, he would be climbing into bed.

Otis greeted them at a side entrance. His thick, flared sideburns and waxed moustache seemed a remnant of another era. He had prepared a tub of popcorn for Pete and Adam.

"Sit anywhere you like," Otis said. He handed them popcorn, soda and two candy bars each.

As a reminder to Hannah of his generosity, he whispered into her ear, "I really shouldn't be doing this." He cast her a wary eye. "This whole notion—your idea. But I'll be the one the boys hate."

Hannah settled in a few seats away from the boys. Otis was heard climbing the stairs to the projection booth.

The movie began.

Stomping loudly on the stairs, Otis returned to the lobby. Twenty minutes into the movie, he tiptoed back upstairs to the projection booth. He turned off the sound and silently returned to the lobby.

Adam and Pete looked at one another, first in astonishment, then agitation. They shifted in their seats, looking at Hannah and then spinning around to stare at the projection booth.

"What's happening?" Adam called across to Hannah.

"I'm not sure."

"Where's the sound?" chimed in Pete.

"Why don't you go see if you can find Otis," Hannah suggested.

The boys jumped up and ran to the lobby where they saw Otis seated next to the bathroom, smoking a cigar.

"Hey!" Pete yelled.

"There's no sound."

"How are we supposed to know what's going on?"

Otis jumped up. "No sound?"

"Yeah."

"We'll fix that," promised Otis. "Sorry. It happens from time to time."

Adam considered throwing out a few cuss words.

"Go back to your seats," encouraged Otis. "I'll rewind the reel. We'll get everything in running order. You'll get to see your Batboy." He disappeared through the door to the upper level.

Adam grabbed a pair of candy bars from behind the snack counter.

Otis made a fuss of rewinding the film. "Is this where it cut out?" he called to the boys through the projection window.

"No. Before then."

"Further back."

Otis played a short snippet. "Here?"

"No. More!"

"Is this the spot?"

"That's fine," Adam said, kicking the back of the chair.

The movie continued uneventfully for another seventy-five minutes. Nearing the conclusion, in the midst of constructing a Super Molecular Dust Separator, the sound cut out once again.

Both boys screamed simultaneously.

Otis rushed into the theater. "What's wrong?"

"It happened again!" Pete yelled.

After several minutes of trouble-shooting the projector, Otis announced, "It can't be fixed. Not until tomorrow."

Adam let out a long groan, letting Otis know just how upset he was.

"Do you want to watch the ending or not?"

The boys watched the last nine minutes of the movie in silence.

On the drive home, the boys barely spoke a word. What should have been a lively discussion was sullen silence.

From time to time, Adam looked at Hannah, beginning to entertain the idea that she was somehow responsible for the mishap. "I think Otis was feeding us a pack of lies," Adam ventured under his breath.

For her part, Hannah was beginning to question her role in the evening. Had she miscalculated. Were her intentions misguided? Would the scheme backfire?

*****

*****

The knock on Nathan's apartment door was both timid and insistent.

"Hannah, what's wrong?" Nathan asked, seeing her troubled expression.

For a moment Hannah was unable to speak.

"It's Five Paws," she whispered.

"Is he not doing well?"

"Would you be willing to drive us to the vet? I'd like to hold him. I know it's a lot to ask."

"No, not at all," Nathan insisted. "Get Five Paws. I'll meet you at the van."

On his drive around the complex, he stopped briefly at the supply closet. He pulled up next to the Metro, leaned over and opened the door for Hannah.

After picking up the main road, heading toward Willmar, Nathan asked, "How did Five Paws get his name?"

"Whether he was born with a short tail or some barn rat bit off the tip when he was a kitten, it looked like he had three back paws when he sat with his tail curled up beside him."

Five Paws looked up, as if to correct Hannah. "Five, thank you very much, not three. Never three." He licked Hannah's hand.

"The vet thought an infusion of fluid under his skin might revive him, but he keeps falling over. To the left. A slow, teetering collapse."

Nathan reached over and stroked Five Paws on the head, who looked up and licked his hand.

"He likes you. Even more than Darla who feeds him endless treats."

When Hannah was ushered into Doctor Wenger's office and sat down in a corner chair, nothing needed to be said other than, "It's time."

"We can administer the pentobarbital on our own, or you can hold him. Whichever…."

"Oh, I'll hold him. He needs to be held."

"We'll get a towel, to place under him."

"I understand," Hannah said. "He may soil himself."

Doctor Wenger left the room. Hannah waited, wishing to feel the hand of Horace on her shoulder. Several moments later an assistant entered and with an electric clippers shaved Five Paws front right foreleg. Doctor Wenger returned with a syringe, pulled up a chair and slipped the needle in place. Gently, he placed the stethoscope against the heart of Five Paws and waited. Listening.

—*Sitting on the narrow shelf, batting the pencil as Hannah tallied up the day's earnings.*

—*Reaching inside the heating vent, pawing, certain it was home to a family of mice.*

—*Rubbing his right cheek against the doorknob while Darla scratched his rump.*

—*The last, slow survey of the supply-filled store before falling asleep.*

—*Standing, slapping his tail against the chamber pot anytime Hannah relieved herself.*

—*The three a.m. yowl, as piercing as a rooster's crow.*

Gone.

"He's gone," Doctor Wenger whispered. He stood up. "Take as much time as you need. We can look after his remains or…."

"No," Hannah said. "I will see to his final resting place."

She carried her lifeless companion outside to the car where Nathan waited.

"I'm sorry," Nathan said. He turned on the engine and they began their journey home. As they approached the turnoff road to the lodge, Nathan continued onward.

"Where are we going?" asked Hannah.

"The only place that makes any sense."

He parked his car by the Mercer graveyard, got out and retrieved a shovel from the trunk.

Hannah slipped out of the passenger seat. "How did you know?"

"I didn't. But we're in the right place, aren't we?"

"Yes. Yes, we are."

Hannah stood to the side while Nathan dug the grave for Five Paws. It was far deeper than it needed to be, but they understood one another perfectly. Five Paws would not be a sacrifice to any scavenging animal.

"Do you have a blanket in the car, Nathan, that you could spare?"

Nathan shook his head.

"We can't bury Five Paws like this. He needs a shroud." Hannah looked around, thinking. "If you would, turn your back for a moment."

Nathan obliged.

Hannah removed her dress and slip, then quickly stepped back into her dress. "It's okay, Nathan. I'm finished." She wrapped Five Paws in her slip and placed him in the ground.

Nathan filled in the grave as Hannah watched in silence. He found a large stone nearby and placed it over the freshly-turned earth.

"There's no one left." Hannah said. "No one who shared life with me on the farm."

Nathan nodded. Hannah took his hand and together they walked from under the shade of *Periscope* into the muted sun.

*****

*****

Hearing the desperation in Naomi's voice, Hannah consented to meet the deacon's wife at the Adele laundromat on Saturday morning.

"You're a doll," Naomi swooned when Hannah walked through the door; she was pouring two large boxes of *Rit* powder dye into an oversize washing machine.

"What are you doing?" inquired Hannah.

"There is too much white in our house. I told Eli, 'All the whiteness is driving me bonkers.' He just stared at me. Like a bleached prune. This crazed look. Astonished, with a tinge of disgust. 'You need sun,' I told him. 'Go for a walk, get some color!'" She wiped her nose. "So, I'm dyeing the living room curtains red!"

"Wouldn't it have been easier to do this at home?" asked Hannah.

"Well, I wasn't about to use my washer. Dye is nasty stuff. For weeks, it tints everything it touches. Eli sporting pink undies would be an awful blessed sight." She opened a third box of dye and poured it into the drum. "Sometimes, I think he thinks I'm mental."

Hannah threw aside a magazine and sat down.

Naomi slammed the lid shut, spun the temperature dial and punched the start button. "Thanks, Hannah," she said, turning in place. She sat next to Hannah, dropped her head and looked over the rim of her glasses. "It's that time of year again."

"Time of year?"

"For Eli to go to another one of those church conferences."

"Oh. Yes. Where is it this year?"

"Dallas."

"Maybe he'll come back with a little bit of color."

"He leaves Wednesday."

"You don't seem none too disappointed."

"I've rented a convertible. The minute Eli leaves I'm heading for Las Vegas."

"By yourself?"

"I've asked Larry. But he's been dragging his feet. Still, I'm going. With or without him!"

"What are you planning to do in Las Vegas?"

"Anything and everything I can't do here!"

"Oh, Naomi, you sure are determined to make a go at it," chuckled Hannah.

"It may not be Paris. But it's a city of lights. And I'm good at pretending."

Naomi jumped up and grabbed a wicker picnic basket resting on a folding table. "I guess you wouldn't be interested in going if Larry gives me the boot?"

"No. But I'd like to hear all about it when you return."

Naomi opened the basket lid and pulled out several Tupperware containers. "I brought us the fixings for French Meringue Cake Merveilleux!" She snapped off a lid and withdrew a meringue round and placed it delicately on a glass cake stand with a trumpet stem. "Nobody in Las Vegas will know I'm a Mennonite." She spread several scoops of toffee cream from another container over the meringue. "Nobody will look at me and think of Eli." She placed a second round of meringue atop the cream and covered it, then licked her fingers. "Nobody will say, 'Oh, that's the deacon's wife, the malcontent.'" The layered cake was crowned with a sprinkling of shaved chocolate. "I'll be free as a bird. If only for a few days." She cut a slice for Hannah and herself. "When I'm gone, can you stop by the house? Check in on the garden, water the plants, pick up the mail?"

"I'd be glad to," Hannah said.

"The Maidenhair Fern likes to be watered daily. I don't care if any of them die. Except for the Maidenhair." She swallowed hard, remembering its history.

"I'll stop by daily. That's a promise."

"I don't trust anyone else to do it. I could ask Larry if he stays back, but, really, I can't run the risk of his being seen around the house."

"I understand. What exactly is going on between Larry and you?"

"I don't know what it is about Larry. Something keeps holding him back."

"I've always liked Larry. I find him honest."

"What about Nathan?" asked Naomi. "What's his story?"

"He very much enjoys living by himself."

"He's not the dating type?"

Hannah smiled. "There's nothing stopping you from finding out, is there?"

*****

*****

The three chairs, carefully and fully wrapped in padded comforts, were loaded into the Metro. To keep them from shifting on the drive to Willmar they were lashed into place with a clothes line. Velma climbed into the passenger seat, dumped several *Chiclets* into the palm of her hand and chucked them into her mouth. Hannah settled back and clutched the steering wheel. It was difficult to tell who was more anxious.

"I think this is the first time I've seen you in a dress," remarked Hannah as she shifted into reverse.

"Don't get used to the look," Velma snorted.

The interior was filling up with the smell of fresh varnish.

"If you don't like what I've done," Velma said, holding her breath, "I'll start over."

"I'm not worried. You shouldn't be either."

"It's a very personal thing," Velma acknowledged. "Knowing you. Making something to honor your family."

"Not just for me," Hannah added.

Velma threw her a puzzled look.

"You, as well," Hannah continued. "You're the artist. It's personal for you, too."

"But I didn't know your husband. Or your sons."

"What you mean is you never met them."

Velma contemplated Hannah's remarks for a moment. "Some people would say what I do is craft. Not art."

Hannah grunted. "That would be a good question for Horace, although I suspect I know what he'd say."

"You are not bound to like them, Hannah," insisted Velma. "I mean it. I can redesign them."

When they arrived at the Ruston County Branch Library, Vivian was waiting for them. She ran down the steps and took Hannah's arm, guiding her to the curb.

"This is the first time I've seen you in overalls," Hannah said, smiling broadly.

Velma joined the pair and they headed up the steps. Inside, with the door closed, Velma and Vivian kissed each other on the lips.

"I been missing that," Velma said.

Vivian turned to Hannah. "You must be so excited. And maybe a little nervous?"

"I have yet to see the chairs. It's all been a secret."

Vivian and Velma exchanged knowing looks.

"You've cheated! Both of you. Girls!"

"Maybe I've seen a thing or two," Vivian joked.

"It feels like a conspiracy. Sharing secrets. Keeping me in the dark."

"Well, the mystery is about to end."

Vivian and Velma marched outside, pulling Hannah along behind them. They opened the Metro door, undid the cord and carried the chairs into the lobby of the library.

They grew silent.

Throughout the many months while Velma was constructing the chairs, it was no secret that Vivian and Velma had pumped Hannah for information about her family. There was no pretense; the pair pried shamelessly. In the process the trio had come to know a great deal about each other.

"The question is: who unwraps them?"

"Hannah. Without a doubt."

"Velma. It's her vision. Her handiwork."

"It's a gift to the library. Vivian."

"There's really only once solution," offered Hannah. "We each unwrap one."

Without uttering a word, they each knew it was the right answer.

Velma was the first to volunteer.

The chair was a simple design, inspired by a French Art Deco version that Vivian had found while searching a series of books on period furniture. Built from oak, it has saber legs and an open frame back that held two curved, horizontal panels –

a wide upper band and below that a narrow rib. A relief had been carved by Velma into the wide panel.

Hannah stepped forward to observe the scene. The keys of a piano, rendered in an enhanced perspective, fanned out from the center. From between the cracks of the keys, plants sprouted upward: wheat, corn, sprigs of clover. Their stalks intertwined. The more mature plants were shedding seeds that rose upward. The seeds in flight transformed into a chorus of musical notes. Below the keys, barely discernible, were a network of roots, some delicate and searching, others strong and set. Across the bottom, in raised letters, one could read:

> *Even in winter, it shall be green in my heart.*
> *Frédéric Chopin.*

"Horace," Hannah whispered, running her hand over the letters. "It can't be improved."

Gently, Velma spun the chair around to reveal a small, engraved brass plaque on the back:

Horace Mercer 1924 - 1961.

Except for the relief, the second chair was an exact replica of the first. On the panel, barely visible was a large hand, fingers splayed widely. Using the fingers and thumb as anchors, Charlotte had spun an elaborate, elastic web. The strands were made of brass wire, flattened and placed edgewise into narrow channels cut in the wood. In the center of the web, as though he were resting on a hammock of golden lace, lay Wilbur, carefree and content.

> *With the right words, you can change the world.*
> *E. B. White*

"Vivian is responsible for selecting the quotes," offered Velma, placing her arm around her.

"I know who that hand belongs to," Hannah said, fighting back tears. She walked behind the chair and pressed her palm against the plaque:

Simon Mercer 1954 – 1961.

The third chair was a brother to its companions. The same wood. The same frame and simple, honest silhouette. The relief included a Stockman pocketknife with a rippled bone handle. All its blades were visible: a blade at each end, fully extended, and the third, longest blade, open at a less severe angle. In the center a flourishing structure was in the process of being built from Lincoln Logs. Surrounding the building, lying on the ground, were a network of beams, unhewn tree trunks and logs stripped of their bark.

Surely, it was inspired by a story Hannah had related to Velma. Gerald had a set of Lincoln Logs which occupied hours of his childhood. As his structures became more complex, Gerald wished for more supplies. Rather than ask his parents to buy a second set, he crafted his own logs, connectors and planks. From small branches, he constructed the logs, sizing them and whittling out the notches with his pocket knife. Soon he was building elaborate forts, trading posts and traveling accommodations for Lewis and Clark.

> *All I have learned, I learned from books.*
> *Abraham Lincoln.*

Hannah inspected the last plaque:

Gerald Mercer 1952 – 1961.

"From what I've heard of your sons, Gerald would be most like you," Velma said.

Vivian stiffened, fearing Velma's remark might offend Hannah.

Hannah considered. "I never stopped to think of it in that way. You love your children the same, of course. And I imagine what my boys would be like today. What they look like. Who would outrun the other? How they would fill their free time. But, who might be most like me?" After a moment, she shook her head, "I think you're right, Velma. I think it would be Gerald."

*****

*****

On Fridays at noon Hannah suspended her business for an hour to listen to *Kalb County Speaks*. Parking the Metro on a side street or along a dirt road, she would open a bottle of coke and turn on the radio. Today she had backed the Metro into a slot on the perimeter of the A&P parking lot.

Nathan's guest was Martha Bentley.

"Miss Bentley is this year's poet laureate of Kalb County," Nathan announced. "For those interested, Miss Bentley will be giving a reading of her works tomorrow night at the Kalb County Fair. Welcome, Martha."

"You can call me Grandma Martha."

"So you won't mind if I mention your age?"

"Eighty-four," Martha announced, jumping Nathan to the reveal. "I feel like I'm a sister to Grandma Moses, but she paints."

"Grandma Moses didn't start painting until late in life?"

"Exactly! Seventy-eight. I didn't begin writing poetry until I was sixty-two."

"Martha will be reading several poems today." He moved the microphone closer to Martha.

"This first one is based on a painting, *Lord Heal the Child*." Martha paused, then cleared her throat.

> The songs and scenes of childhood
> Mirrored in a Benton painting
> Still vivid after all these years
> Despite time's relentless tainting.
>
> Did Benton know on his imagined canvas
> He showed a portrait of my family tree
> And among the fervent crowd
> That little girl on his bench is me?

"Would that be Thomas Hart Benton?" Nathan asked.

"Yes. He loved Missouri. Like me."

Though Hannah was looking at folks entering and leaving A&P, she saw a child from the past surrounded by her parents.

"Do you know the mural in the main hall of the State Capital in Jefferson City is by Benton?"

Nathan replied, "I've seen it."

"'His best work,' Benton called it. He was a very talented painter. But he was a bit of a scoundrel, too."

"Oh. How so?"

"He said some very unkind words about the men who run museums."

Nathan encouraged her. "I'm sure our listeners would like to know."

"I'm here to read poetry, not gossip," Martha retorted.

"How does one become a poet laureate?"

"I have no idea. I give out copies whenever I can. Here and there. The coffee shop. The clerks at the drug store. My butcher. And the next thing you know, I get a letter from the Arts Council!"

"Are you published?"

"Oh goodness no. I'm not *that* good."

"For those who just tuned in, we are talking to Martha Bentley, Poet Lauerate of Kalb County."

"This is entitled *Doll*. I don't think it needs an explanation. A doll is a doll is a doll."

> From a scrap of cloth she was contrived;
> To her, a secret name was ascribed.
> The cynic says she hasn't any heart,
> No repertoire of words to impart.
> Her stuffing is a silly substitute for bones
> Her eyes are simply polished stones.
> But, to me, she is portal to countless magic rooms
> A thousand roles my cherished doll assumes.
> When I am low, short on dreams, without desire
> She fuels my heart. She warms me with her fire.

"It seems your childhood plays an important role in your poetry."

"That, and celebrating the land." Martha extended her hands. "This dirt under my fingernails? I've always had it."

"You may have just penned a title for you next poem," Nathan said.

"Oh, I like you," Martha laughed. "You get it!"

"Simple words," Hannah thought, "placed in the right order...." The muscles tightened in her chest.

"I had no intention of reading this next poem," Martha said. "But on the drive over here it was so pretty I got to thinking about all the people who've never been to Missouri and what they're missing."

There was an abrupt pause.

"No! I wasn't driving," Martha exclaimed. "Pauline brought me."

"And Pauline is...?"

"The butcher! As I was saying. It was such a beautiful drive. And I thought of my child. He was stillborn. I was twenty-three so that was, what? Sixty one years ago?" She sighed, then whispered the title, *To a Child Born Still*.

What doors – now closed – were built for you?
What windows – forever shut – were framed within
    your house?
What landscapes embraced your sweet domain.

To give this mystery meaning,
What equation shall his father navigate?
What ancient sage shall his mother quote?

Shall we say that life
Is the taking, taking, taking
Of all things given
And you were wise to pass it by?

Shall we admit we hold
No means to brace the winds

That will surely wrest your soul
And you were no fool to refuse us?

Shall we lament your choice,
Knowing, despite the taking,
In spite of etching winds,
You would have liked it here.

For the first time, Hannah wept, truly, deeply wept for the losses of her life.

*****

*****

The new house would be built beside Velma's woodworking shop. Hannah was chosen to break ground; there was no runner-up.

It was not a traditional ceremony. In place of a shovel, Velma squatted and held a dull wedge upright while Hannah struck it with a forged hammer — both instruments from Velma's grandfather's tool collection.

Vivian adjusted her scarf.

Velma placed her arm around Vivian's shoulder. "Home," she whispered.

Vivian nodded. Her mother, Nattie, was gone. *Home.* A dream that reached back to her childhood. A mother, who was entrusted to provide one, had failed to do so. Now she had a place with Velma.

Velma turned to Hannah. "How do you like living in the cottage?"

"I'm still getting used to it."

"Does this mean you'll stay here come winter?" asked Vivian.

"I haven't decided, but I think I'll go south," Hannah said. "I still feel like a bird."

*****

*****

There was a bountiful outpouring of cherries the spring of 1967. They were not just model specimens of fruit, but jolly bellies, plump with flavor and juice.

Dewey insisted Hannah deliver a half-bushel of the morsels to Frank, whose farm was only a few miles from the hotel. Hannah phoned ahead and promised, if Laverne could gather together the equipment, she would help can the cherries.

The deterioration of Norma, who had been confined to bed over the past winter was shocking.

Hannah pulled a chair next her. There were fresh flowers and a pitcher of iced water on the bedside table.

Stroking Norma's hand, Hannah said, "You must tell me if there's anything I can do to help."

Norma responded with a weak, angelic smile. "Thank you, Hannah, dear."

Laverne could be heard clinking jars together in the kitchen. Cupboard doors being opened and closed. Paring knives and stirring spoons assembled on the table.

"Please don't tell Frank," Norma whispered, "but I don't think I have much fight left in me."

"Canned cherries last a long, long time," Hannah said. "They love to be eaten with a simple custard and cinnamon. You can't let them down."

Norma inclined her head towards Hannah. "Do you think Frank will marry Laverne?"

"Oh, Norma. You can't let yourself think such thoughts."

"I want Frank to remarry. I told him."

"Frank loves you!" Hannah said sternly. "We'll have no more of this talk."

"I know he loves me." She looked out the window. "A man capable of loving shouldn't be denied *from* loving."

Hannah rose and said simply, "Why don't you rest? I'll be sure to step in and say goodbye before I leave."

"I'm only sorry I couldn't give him children."

Hannah raised her eyebrows. There was something unsettling in the way Norma worded her desire.

"What about you, Hannah? Will you remarry?"

"Aren't you the curious one?"

"How long has it been?"

"Nearly six years."

"Horace was a loving man, too. Frank and Horace. They seemed more than neighbors, like brothers. I said that more than once."

"Hush, now" Hannah said. "Don't over-exert yourself."

"Why does it upset you when I say that?"

"Laverne is waiting," Hannah said. She kissed Norma on the forehead.

Since their trip to St. Louis, Laverne and Hannah had never spoken of the incident, of the trip, of the abortion. Nor did they today. They pitted and canned fourteen quarts of cherries, steeped in rich syrup.

Frank stopped by briefly to thank Hannah.

Laverne offered him a handful of cherries to sample.

"How's Dewey?" he asked.

"I don't see him very much," Hannah admitted. "I mainly do business with his wife."

There was the customary talk of the weather, then Frank left.

When Hannah went to say goodbye to Norma, she found her sleeping peacefully. She decided to visit the family gravesite, then return to wish Norma well.

Walking up the hill, approaching *Periscope*, she recalled Norma's words, "*I'm only sorry I couldn't give him children.*" For Hannah, giving birth was neither an expectation nor a duty. It was a mutual choice made in love. Simon and Gerald were a gift to herself as much as to her husband. Hannah knew she was being unfair to Norma; she didn't mean what she implied.

She was simply giving voice to centuries-old proclamations of men who claimed to stand between women and God.

Nearing the gravesite, Hannah couldn't help but think that Horace had a reverence that far surpassed that of Deacon Stahl....

She stopped in shock at the scene before her. The tombstone of Horace had been pushed over. The headstone of Simon was cracked in two, the broken half lying on the ground. A large portion of Gerald's stone had been shattered, pieces scattered over his grave.

She sank to her knees, one hand resting on the inscribed letters of her husband's name.

After a long cry of broken sobs, then quiet disbelief, she gathered the broken pieces and laid them next to the trunk of *Periscope*. She managed to upright the headstone of Horace by packing dirt around its base. Slowly, she made her way back to Frank and Norma's farm.

Laverne met her at the door. "Norma's awake now. She'd love to see you."

"I can't see her just now," Hannah said. "I'm sorry. Tell her I'm sorry."

*****

*****

"I have news!" Wanda exclaimed before the door to the office of *Cantor's Warehouse and Supply Center* had closed behind Hannah. Jumping up, the receptionist ran around the counter and enveloped Hannah with a huge hug. She stepped back and twirled, keeping her hands behind her back and thrusting her belly forward.

"Can you see a difference?"

Hannah gave Wanda a once-over. "New shoes?"

"I'm pregnant!"

"That's wonderful news," Hannah replied, prompted by Wanda's excitement.

"That's not all!"

Hannah clapped her hands together in anticipation.

Wanda displayed her left hand which sported a large moonstone ring.

"I'm engaged!"

"You're just full of surprises."

"The diamond comes later."

"I had no idea."

"There's more," squealed Wanda.

"More?" Hannah said. "Should I sit down?"

"I'm quitting!"

Apparently, Hannah wasn't able to contain her disappointment as she said, "You're leaving *Cantor's*?"

"Don't be sad. This is not the end of us!"

At Mollie's Diner, Wanda brought Hannah up to date on all her exploits. "Remember Maddie?"

"Of course. Hand Grenade Maddie. How could I forget?"

"Well, after I phoned Maddie we reconnected. It turned out Maddie has a brother, Derek. I guess I sorta knew all along, but you know how high school is. All those parties and that grappling for the spotlight and sorting out friends and freaks and mean-ass bitches."

Hannah nodded, not really understanding the world described by Wanda.

Wanda grew serious. "You have no idea how much that night affected me, Hannah. Getting to meet LeRoy and Ethel and little Sammy. And seeing the shit they had to go through, thrown at them by white folks like us."

"Not all white folks!" corrected Hannah.

"Okay, so you're excused. But I was a real prick back in the day. Not just naïve. I'm talking racist. Anyway, Derek's not just a sweet squeeze. He's hip to what's going on in this country."

"He makes you happy. I can tell."

"So, we're going to Mississippi this summer, before I'm too far along, to help register black people to vote. And hell if we're going to let what happened to Chaney and Schwerner and Goodman stop us!"

"Were they the young men murdered by the KKK?"

"Yeah. Investigating a church burning and arrested and turned over to the Klan by a cold-blooded, chicken-shit sheriff. That was '64. And here we are now. It's taken three years to put them on trial. And guess what. The jury is all white. Not a single black person will have a say in the matter!"

"May I tell LeRoy?" asked Hannah. "He'd be so proud of you!"

"Of course!"

"When I first met you," Hannah said, "you said you wanted to be a pilot. And now you will be."

*****

*****

There would be no family meal. Frances had asked Quincy to take Darla and Adam to Willmar and have dinner there, at Russel's Restaurant.

For Hannah, there was leftover stew, heated and served in a green Fiesta bowl, and cornbread. Frances wasn't planning to eat. The pair remained in the kitchen, Hannah seated at a small table, empty bowl pushed aside, Frances standing, leaning against the counter.

"Darla's so happy to be traveling with you again, but Quincy and I still think we should limit her outings to one day a week."

"You know best," Hannah said. "Regardless, it's nice having her back."

"We were curious. Where did you get this book?" She held up *Sign Language* by E. Benson.

Hannah saw it had been torn apart, along the spine, and taped back together.

"My friend Vivian found it."

"It certainly has gotten Darla excited, learning all the signs in it."

"Someone put a lot of work into drawing and explaining them."

"Darla says you're learning them, too."

"I try."

"Vivian, you say?"

"A librarian."

"What made her think of such a book?"

"It's a bit embarrassing," Hannah admitted. "I was leaving Kresge's parking lot, writing a note to Darla, when I hit a guard post rounding a corner. I said, there's got to be a better way for me to communicate my ideas."

"I was wondering how the fender got pushed in like that. Darla claimed she didn't know."

"It's a bit of a mess, isn't it, but I'm thinking of buying a new truck."

"Darla is playing teacher, trying to get us to learn the gestures and meanings."

"That's good, isn't it?"

"Like you, I'm trying," Frances said. "Adam doesn't appreciate being treated like a pupil."

"He still resents his sister?"

Frances picked up the empty bowl and placed it in the sink. Her tone softened, "I have to be fair with Adam. The truth is, I do pay more attention to Darla. I suspect he can't help noticing."

"Has it caused problems between Quincy and you?"

"I would be lying if I said it hadn't."

Hannah brushed aside a few cornbread crumbs. "I think maybe it's best if we not see each other for a while. Give you and your family time to sort things out."

"No!" Frances was quick to reply. "That's not what I want. Darla needs you. I'm not willing to break that relationship. And I'm not going to let this setback ruin our friendship." She walked to the refrigerator, opened it and looked blindly at its contents. Slowly she closed the door and turned to Hannah, "This is very very hard to say."

She came and sat next to Hannah, but found it impossible to look in her eyes. "Darla thinks it was Adam who vandalized the tombstones."

"Did Adam admit to it?"

"No. It's only a hunch on Darla's part."

Hannah nodded.

"Did Darla tell you she suspected Adam?" asked Frances.

"She mentioned it."

"And you didn't say anything to me?!"

"Like you said. It's a guess on Darla's part. Only a guess."

"I have to know," Frances said. "Every time I look at Adam I'm searching for clues, listening for a sign, did you or didn't you? How can I be a mother if I'm so rattled with suspicion? We have to get this out in the open."

Hannah resisted, but Frances pleaded with her to stay and have a talk with Adam, Quincy and her.

When Quincy and the children returned from dinner in Willmar, Darla was sent to her room.

The doors to the living room were closed.

Frances sat forward in an armchair, leaning into Adam who sat alone on the sofa. Quincy and Hannah chose wooden straight-back chairs in the far corners of the room.

"Adam," Frances began, "your father and I love you very much. We're asking you to be completely honest with us tonight."

Adam shifted his eyes side to side; his jaw tightened.

"We all know someone damaged the headstones of Gerald and Simon and Hannah's husband, Horace."

Quincy, sounding formal, asked, "Were you responsible?"

Adam looked up. "Is that another one of Darla's stories?"

"We simply want to know the truth."

"Darla makes things up. And you believe her."

Frances lowered her voice. "Were you the one who did it?"

Adam shared looks with his parents. "Hannah hates me!"

"Hannah doesn't hate you, Adam," Frances said, trying to reassure him.

Adam now looked directly at Hannah. "Hannah thinks it was me. She told you!"

"Adam," Hannah said, "I don't hate you! I love your entire family, including you."

"You love Darla! You hate me!"

Frances looked at Quincy, not knowing what to say or how to proceed.

Hannah stood up and took a seat besides Adam. "Adam, I want to ask for your forgiveness for something I did last year. When I took Pete and you to see that movie, it was a trick. An unfair trick played at your expense. I thought, maybe, by watching a portion of the movie without sound you would understand more what it is like to be Darla, to be deaf. But I was wrong. It was unkind. I am sorry."

Adams shoulders softened.

"You were clever," Hannah continued. "Driving home after the movie I kept thinking, Adam knows what I've been up to."

"That is no reason to destroy something."

"I hope you can forgive me," whispered Hannah.

Adam didn't respond.

"Pete is your friend," Hannah said. "How would you feel if someone hurt Pete. Or broke the things that belonged to him?"

The look in Adam's eyes betrayed him.

"Was it Pete?" Quincy asked.

Adam nodded his head. "I told him to," he said.

"Were you there?" Frances asked.

"I stayed on my bike, by the road, looking out for anybody who might drive by."

"I'm sorry," Frances said to Hannah.

"You can't blame Pete," Adam said, beginning to weep. "He didn't even know about the place until I showed him."

*****

*****

Farm For Sale

Hannah thought of Martha Bentley, the poet laureate, wondering how she would describe *For Sale* in words. Crossing over the Williams' bridge, she felt an affection for the plank that had served a noble purpose in thwarting a band of heartless thugs.

"Why now?" Hannah asked LeRoy, "Just when you've got the farm back into running order?"

"Detroit," LeRoy said with a sparkle in his eye.

"There's farms in Detroit?"

"There's music in Detroit," LeRoy responded.

Hannah understood.

"I sent a few of my songs to Fortune Records. They're interested."

"I listen to the radio on my rounds," Hannah said.

"I waited a long time," LeRoy said. "Record producers and DJ's are finally playing my type of song. Not sugar words and young love. Songs about our people. Songs crying out for change."

Hannah smiled. "Soon I'll be listening to you."

"Me and your husband's guitar."

"How long have you lived here?" asked Hannah.

"Since 1963."

"That's five years." Hannah's eyes welled up. "I know a good auctioneer," she said. "His name is Nathan. He'll treat you right."

*****

*****

Hannah unloaded the entire contents of her truck into the garage of Velma and Vivian's new home. All morning they unpacked the Metro, removing the inventory, as well as the cabinets, shelves and old, modified dressers.

"Can you imagine? From '61 to '68, I drove this contraption all over Kalb County, down to Florida and back, into St. Louis. It's been my home for six of those seven years."

With a hollow-sounding Metro, Hannah drove to Willow Tree Apartments and picked up Larry.

"Afternoon," Larry said, settling into the passenger seat.

"How's your arm?"

"The cast comes off in a week."

"Thank you for doing this, Larry," Hannah said.

"Not a problem."

"You're the expert. Whatever you recommend, that's what I'll buy."

"You know I can't do a test drive," Larry said.

"I'm aware of that. But you have a good ear for engines and know how to kick a tire."

Larry laughed.

"How is the music coming along?

"That sorta came to an end," Larry said, "after the accident."

"It'll come back, don't you think?"

"I'm lucky I didn't kill anyone, Hannah. The woman I hit had three kids in the car."

"I heard."

"You have one noisy truck here," Larry remarked.

"It sounds a lot different empty than it did full."

"I've started going to Creekside. Have you heard?"

"No. I haven't."

"Isn't that your church?"

"I grew up going there, but I wouldn't call it my church."

"If I take up music again," Larry said, "it'll be gospel."

"I must have memorized a hundred hymns in church," Hannah said. "They never go away."

For several miles they drove in silence.

Larry announced, "Drinking. And all that stuff that goes with it… is behind me."

Several more miles of quiet, broken only by the vibrating panels of the Metro.

"Did I tell you my friend LeRoy has gone to Detroit, hoping to cut a record?"

"No! LeRoy?! Good for him."

Larry selected a new 1968 GMC Boyertown panel step van. Satisfied with the trade-in value of the Metro, Hannah paid cash and drove off the lot in command of her new vehicle.

Rather than escaping to Florida that winter, she spent the time with Velma and Vivian preparing the truck for its upcoming, inaugural season.

*****

*****

Every fall the Ruston County School Board hosts a spelling bee, jamboree and dance at Willmar Fire Station and Hall. To make room for the jubilant crowds, the fire trucks are rolled out and parked in the old station, a block away. A stage is erected against the far wall, opposite the huge, rollup doors. Festivities begin at three in the afternoon and last until midnight. This year the hall was decorated to celebrate the recent Apollo 11 moon landing on July 20, 1969.

Darla was hired to cover the event and take formal photographs, as well as candid shots. At eighteen, Darla was an undeniably elegant, gorgeous woman. Hannah and Darla arrived early so Darla could set up a small photo booth which she had prepared for any romantic couples among the crowd seeking a memento of the night. Using stems of wheat, Darla had braided hearts and painted them red. She attached small bouquets of dried clover, tied with lace ribbons. Feathers arranged to look like butterflies and glued to spring-sprung clothes pins were clamped to a simple garden archway. Frances, Quincy and Adam would arrive later, after evening chores, when things were well underway. It seemed Adam, at last, had put his rebellious phase behind him.

A better chaperon for the late-night dance could not have been found than the scripture-quoting Hugo Blackwell. The week after the event, if anyone wanted a postmortem account of inaudible conversations or unseen indiscretions, they could be regaled at Hugo's General Store.

The happenings began with a Marine-Guard salute to the flag followed by the pledge of allegiance and a prayer asking for the Lord's blessing.

The kickoff number was a skit put together by Willmar High School teachers who shamelessly considered themselves thespians. The format was fixed. Entitled *The Wizard of Willard*, the piece was a version of *The Wizard of Oz*, inspire′ by events of the past year.

Anyone who thought they might be the object of ridicule, or who longed to see their rivals ribbed, showed up.

Many of the party-goers knew Hannah: there was no shortage of people to chat with. Throughout the evening, as she circulated among the crowd, she noticed a group of boys hanging around Darla. Some seemed baffled, almost angry, that Darla didn't speak to them. There were a few feeble gestures, awkward attempts to prompt her to speak. When she signaled her deafness, they mirrored her gesture, followed by raised hands. Were they mocking her? Was it harmless flirtation?

A handsome young man with loose curls of black hair and deep dimples seemed to be the ringleader, holding sway over his buddies. Around Darla, however, he seemed to be the shyest of the group.

After hanging with Darla and ogling the couples who posed for photographs, the boys moved on.

During the Junior Spelling Bee Competition, the gang of boys appeared again. To the delight of the crowd, two posed together for a photograph, one on his knee appearing to propose to the other.

Hannah, having purchased a slice of lemon meringue pie from the Junior League Girls Club bake sale, kept a watchful eye on Darla while eating her dessert. She saw Velma, Vivian and Nathan arrive together and went to greet them. Nathan would participate in the Senior Spelling Bee Competition and surely win.

Around nine, members of the *Jaw Harp Band* arrived and began setting up their equipment.

Hugo joined them on stage and admonished everyone, "Abstain from fleshly lusts which are a damnation of the soul."

By the photo booth, the boys had convinced Darla to loan them her camera and for her to pose with the curly-headed lad.

Jaw Harp was the perfect band to elicit dancing. Vivian and Velma took turns dancing with Nathan. Of all the couples, Frances displayed the most graceful moves on the floor, moving with ease and quiet poise as Quincy let himself be guided by his wife.

"May I have this dance?" It was Frank.

Hannah faltered. Had enough time passed since Norma's death to accept his offer? "You may," she said.

From across the room, Darla snapped a picture of the couple, just as Frank wrapped his arm around Hannah's waist.

"How are you doing?" Hannah asked.

"I miss her greatly," Frank said. "But I've known for a long time I'd be here."

"I'm forty-four," Hannah said. "I didn't expect to lose so many people at this stage in my life. That happens later, I thought, when you're eighty-four."

She shifted slightly closer to Frank.

Hugo did not approve.

*****

*****

As midnight approached and *Jaw Harp* announced its closing number, Fire Chief Bix Huntley located and cornered Hannah.

"What's your truck doing parked in front of the old fire station?"

"My truck? What are you talking about? It's parked by the curb, next to the donut shop."

"Maybe it was. Not anymore."

Hannah joined Bix and they walked briskly down the street. "You're sure it's my truck?"

"It has your name on the side. *Hannah's Goods & Effects*. So I'm pretty sure."

When they arrived at the station they discovered the truck raised up on wooden blocks, all four tires removed, lying on the ground next to their hubs.

"Oh, Lord," exclaimed Hannah.

"Any idea what's going on?" asked Bix.

"Who would do such a thing?"

"Well, it's got to be moved. It's blocking the rollup door. If there were a fire, we couldn't get out."

"Whoever did this should put the tires back on and move the truck."

"We don't have time to investigate. It's gotta be moved, Mrs. Mercer. Now!"

"I'm still baffled as to how this could have happened. Where were your men? Didn't they see anybody park the truck and remove the tires?"

"They were up the street. At the dance."

"There was nobody here?"

"Mrs. Mercer, we're a volunteer company. You know we don't have paid staff to man the station 'round the clock."

"What do I do? Call a towing company?"

"Ma'am, my men will put the tires back on and you can be on your way."

"Oh, hell, no they won't!"

Bix was unprepared for Hannah's outburst. "I beg your pardon?"

"This is criminal! Whoever took them off should put them back on!"

"Mrs. Mercer. I think this was probably more of a prank than something criminal. I doubt your truck was damaged."

"This truck is my livelihood. My second home."

"It can't stay here." He radioed for help.

"Here's what we'll do," proposed Hannah, "Put the tires back on. Move the van to the side and take them off again. I'll sleep in the van. I'll wait here until whoever did this shows up and makes it right."

"And how are you going to find the guy who did this?" Bix asked, clearly frustrated.

"I'll contact the television station and have them run a story. Word will get around. Somebody knows something."

"Do listen to reason, Mrs. Mercer."

"My mind's made up, Bix." Darla joined the pair, indicating her decision to stand by Hannah.

The local affiliate was thrilled to broadcast the mysterious incident of the hijacked vehicle. They added their own spin to the drama: Was it possible the escaped inmate from Bedford Prison was the culprit?

The story aired Sunday evening.

Two hours later, there was a knock on Hannah's van door. It was Sheriff Wilson.

"I have someone who wants to see you."

"I'm available," Hannah said.

"You caused a lot of fuss, Mrs. Mercer, for such a little incident."

"Oh? A minor incident?"

"This whole thing was just a couple of boys trying to catch the attention of Darla." He adjusted his cap, then rubbed the back of his neck. "Don't be too hard on him. I hired him to wash the cruisers and he's a right good worker."

The sheriff stepped aside and made room for the curly-headed lad to approach Hannah, who stepped from the van.

"I'm sorry. It was my fault."

"What's your name?" Hannah asked, recognizing his face from the evening before.

"Thomas Nolt."

"Where are the others?"

I guess they were too scared to show."

"Is it true what the sheriff says? You caused this fracas just to catch the attention of Darla?"

"Yeah."

"Well, that's a relief. I thought it was just plain meanness."

Darla emerged, standing in the doorway behind Hannah.

Noting a change in Thomas, Hannah did a halfway turn to see Darla.

"You aim to speak to Darla?" Hannah asked, pulling a pencil and tablet from her pocket.

Thomas shrugged.

"Well, this is how you do it." She handed the tablet to Thomas. "Your name and a simple 'How do you do?'"

"I can't write," Thomas said.

Hannah retracted the pen and tablet. She wrote, "My name is Thomas." She handed the tablet back to Thomas. "Go on, show her."

Thomas showed the note to Darla who smiled and nodded her head.

"Anything else you want to say?" Hannah asked Thomas.

"No Ma'am."

"Allow me." Once more Hannah jotted something on the tablet. She handed the note to Thomas. "Show Darla."

When she read the note, Thomas was rewarded with a radiant smile from her. He blushed.

Hannah faced Thomas and said, "You just told her she's very pretty." She paused and added, "And that you're going to go to school and learn to write."

Hannah approached Sheriff Wilson and leaned into him. "He can't write?"

"From a young age, Thomas was a ward of the state," Sheriff Wilson explained. "He's one of those cases where someone is left to fend for himself and ends up slipping through the cracks. He's a bright fella, though. Just listen to him juice his buddies."

*****

*****

"Could I convince you to have dinner with me this weekend?"

"Are you asking me on a date, Frank?"

"I suppose I am."

"A fancy meal. Is that what you have in mind?"

"Well, I wasn't thinking *Denny's*."

"When you're ready to harvest another crop of alfalfa, I propose you call me for a date. I know how to drive a tractor. How's that?"

"It's a date."

Two weeks later Hannah commandeered the John Deere, flawlessly guiding the baler pickup with its wheels of spinning spikes over the rows of dried alfalfa. The fodder was compacted into bales, double-tied with twine, and forced out the chute. Frank stood on the flatbed wagon, grabbed the bales and stacked them in interlocking layers.

As Hannah reached the end of each row and spun the tractor around, the couple exchanged smiles. The field yielded two and one-half wagonloads of labor.

Afterwards, the pair sat on the edge of the third wagon. Hannah opened the picnic basket as Frank poured them sweet peppermint water from a thermos.

She handed him a meatloaf sandwich. "This beats fine china and crystal goblets." A moment later she added, "Perhaps I'm being unfair," recalling the tableware she'd sold off years ago. "There's something to be said for that, too."

Frank looked at her with a soft sense of longing.

"Everyone had you married to Laverne," Hannah said. "Including your wife."

"I'm well aware of that."

"What went wrong?"

"There are certain very fine people who just don't affect you in that way." He rested his hand on Hannah's thigh. "I never conceived of asking Laverne for a date."

Hannah rested her hand on top of Frank's. "If we were to see one another, it wouldn't be a betrayal of Norma?"

"You say that... thinking of Horace?"

"It can't be avoided, for either of us, I suppose."

"When all is said and done, isn't it a matter of whether we want our past to control us or not?"

"I suppose," Hannah said, "things can change without ever changing."

"I have something for you," Frank said. He took her hand. They hopped off the wagon and he led her towards the barn. In the corner of the main bay, from a bed of straw, he picked up a kitten and handed it to Hannah. "I think she's been waiting to meet you."

Hannah accepted the kitten and drew it to her chest. She smiled at Frank. "You mean her for me?"

"Absolutely."

She looked down. Although the kitten was silvery gray, around its nose was a teardrop of white. And in the center of its forehead, just above its eyes was a black dot.

Without hesitation, Hannah held the kitten at arm's length and said, "I shall call you *Three Eyes*."

*****

*****

Hannah requested and was awarded a meeting with the Dean of Students at Washburn Art Academy. Rarely did Hannah cancel one of her rounds but this time was an exception. Doctor Philban was only available on Mondays and Thursdays.

Vivian had helped Darla prepare her portfolio, a rich collection of sketches, paintings and photographs. "You may be criticized for not having examples of commercial art," warned Vivian. "There aren't any abstract pieces, either, but some of your photographs aren't purely representational, so that's good."

Darla, who had just turned nineteen, pressed Vivian to explain the differences between various genres of art.

Doctor Philban was not perfunctory. He took ten minutes to study the portfolio while Darla and Hannah sat in silence.

"They're quite good," he said, closing the folder. "Miss Leichty is an accomplished artist." He removed his glasses and began to polish them. "Unfortunately, the academy is not equipped to take non-traditional students."

Hannah offered a small sigh of relief. He hadn't said *abnormal, handicapped, afflicted, disabled, impaired.*

"Doctor Philban, if Darla had the ability to hear, there would be no question. Her application would be accepted?"

"Without a doubt." He replaced his glasses. "She can take consolation in that."

"Perhaps, if you told her directly, Doctor Philban."

Not having determined if Darla could read lips, he wrote her a note.

"When God grants Darla the ability to hear, perhaps we'll return."

"Come now," Dr. Philban said. "Is it fair to ask our instructors to write out everything they say in class?"

"It does require time."

"Doesn't such an expectation strike you as preferential?"

"Excuse me, Dr. Philban," Hannah said, rising. "Let me introduce you to another member of our party." She walked to the door and opened it. In walked Hand-Grenade Maddie who, when preparing for the interview, had proposed to go by an assumed name. "This is Judith Soloway."

Dr. Philban rose but remained behind his desk.

"Judith has agreed to attend classes with Darla and act as her ears."

"I understand. A personal notetaker?"

"She's a professional stenographer. Well trained. Excellent recommendations, and will be paid for her services." Hannah offered a certificate to Dr. Philban. "Would you like to see her diploma?"

"This would be a highly unusual situation. It's never been done."

"But you're a man who embraces the unusual," Hannah said. "I can tell."

The doctor blushed. "Naturally, I would have to take the idea up with the board of directors."

"They can be persuaded," Hannah said. "I don't doubt your abilities for a minute."

"Your name, again?" Dr. Philban asked.

"Hannah Mercer. Let me assure you. Judith knows how to stay in the background. Really. No one will know she's in the room. We'll even manufacture a portable stool for her that she can bring to class."

"I can't make any promises, but I'll do my best.

*****

*****

Thomas Nolt didn't return to school. But he did begin taking lessons, splitting time between Vivian and Hannah. He learned quickest, however, when Nathan joined Hannah in the lobby and provided his own brand of peculiar instruction.

The camel jumped through a hoop of purple burning lilacs

Nathan would write on a large card. It was Thomas' job to act out each word as well as spell it aloud several times.

Laughing hyenas danced on a checkerboard of frozen and roasted circles

"That doesn't make sense," Thomas would say before performing each exercise.

"Why should it?" Nathan replied. "I want you to pay attention to details."

Prior to her visits to St. Louis, Hannah would sit down with Thomas and help him compose a letter to Darla.

Dear Darla, Thank you for the...

"How do you spell photograph?"

"P. H. O. T. O. G. R. A. P. H."

... photograph. Every day, wherever I go, I see pitchers on walls. I never looked before. I like what you draw...

"Does better have one t or two?"

"Two."

... better. Do they have good food in St. Louis? Remember...

"Has Darla had other boyfriends?"

"It is not good or necessary to know all her secrets, Thomas."

"What do girls like more? Makeup or kissing?'

"None of that nonsense. If I like engines and airplanes, does that make me a boy?"

"Does sheriff begin with an s or a c?"

"S"

... Sherif Wilson? He says hello. Now that I am learning to read and write, Hannah says I should ask for a raise. I hope to see you soon. Your dear friend, Thomas.

*****

*****

On Frank's visits to Hannah, rather than park at the hotel, Frank parked in the town of Adele and walked the half-mile, coming in behind the building to avoid being seen by Nathan or anyone in the lobby.

On Hannah's visits to Frank, not wanting to broadcast her whereabouts, she parked the van by the family graveyard and walked through the fields to Frank's farm.

"Do you think Laverne suspects anything?"

With the death of Norma, Laverne's work schedule had been cut back to three days a week; no longer was she spending nights at the farm.

Getting out of bed, Frank said, "To be honest, yes."

"Has she said anything?"

"No."

"I suspect the same of Nathan. He knows."

"Hungry?"

"I could eat something sweet," Hannah said, smiling. She rolled out of bed. "What do you have?"

After pulling on his trousers, Frank turned and kissed Hannah. "Let's go see."

Hannah slipped on her nightgown and paused by the dresser to observe the framed sketches of Frank and Norma, drawn by Darla.

"That was the beginning," she said.

"Does it bother you that I keep them here?"

"No."

"I can move them to another room."

"It doesn't bother me." She noticed a stack of papers by the portraits but paid them no attention. "Every time after we see each other, I think I should start going to church again."

Frank coming up behind Hannah, wrapped his arms around her and kissed the back of her neck.

He said, "You have too much Horace in you to do that."

*****

*****

When Darla became a student at Washburn Art Academy, Hannah decided to drive to St. Louis on Tuesday evenings. She spent Tuesday nights with Wanda, her husband Derek and their son, Elijah. On Wednesdays, Hannah went to *Cantor's* to refresh her stock, then she'd drive back to Adele that afternoon.

"Your replacement is a very sour, angry young woman," Hannah told Wanda. "Hard as I try, she refuses any kind of communication."

Darla and Maddie had joined the gathering and were seated around the table, waiting for Chinese food to be delivered.

"Everybody's angry these days," Maddie declared.

Darla passed about a note. "You'll never guess what happened today in life drawing."

Everyone looked at her in anticipation. Darla indicated Maddie should answer the question.

Maddie blushed. "Flo – and I seriously doubt that's her real name – is one of the regular models. She was scheduled to pose today but didn't show. I could see the instructor, Wade – and I seriously doubt that's his real name – was sorta out-to-sea. So that's when I said, 'I'll pose!'"

"You didn't!" Wanda cried.

"Hey, sister, don't give me that look."

"What look?

"The Wade look. The are-you-serious look. The you-gotta-be-kidding-me-is-this-a-joke, look. What he was really thinking was, sister, you're way too fat to pose nude in my class."

Darla nodded.

"Sorry," Wanda said meekly.

"But the students are into it. I can tell. And Wade is getting the same vibe. So I pulled off my tee-shirt and the kids cheered. No shit. I did a little shimmy. You want it? Sorry,

Derek. Am I embarrassing you? What I got may not be what you're used to, but these boobs are as real as a pair of tits. I took off my bra. I thought, okay, that was easy. Here's the hard part: ripping off my skirt and taking off my panties. But you know what? It was a piece of cake. Nobody was judging. There wasn't any shame and, boy, did I feel liberated! Here is one fat Maddie standing in for Barbie doll Flo and every bit as hot and juicy as that skinny bitch!"

Hannah applauded. Except for Derek, the others joined in.

"Now for the weird part. After class Wade – did I say I seriously doubt that's his real name — comes up to me and he says, 'You were a natural. Would you model again, some time? The pay is good!"

"I wanna see! Darla, did you bring your drawing of Maddie?"

"Eewgh," Derek said.

"For the first time in my life," Maddie said, "I'm gonna eat all the Chinese food I want and not feel guilty about it!"

*****

*****

"Why are we having dinner in the shop?"

"The tree Velma picked out was too tall for the living room," Vivian pointed out. "She refused to saw off the bottom and shorten the trunk."

"It's cozy," Maddie said, laying the six of diamonds on the discard pile. "I especially like the pot belly stove. It has a Santa vibe."

Hannah picked up the six and placed it under the four and five of diamonds, forming a run. She had, once again, decided to remain in Missouri over the winter months after being diagnosed with a mild case of pneumonia in early November 1973.

"When you're through with your game, can you help me set up the tables?" Vivian asked Maddie.

"That's what Thomas is for," Maddie said. She turned so Darla could read her lips and addressed the group of women, "I predict Darla is going to receive a ring for Christmas."

Darla, who was tying small charms to sprigs of pine, blushed.

"She made those in ceramics class."

During Darla's second year at the academy, the need for Maddie to be an interpreter came to an end as the instructors preferred relating directly to Darla. Many loaned her their lecture notes. Maddie was not disappointed; she had discovered a new way to supplement her income.

"Did you hear?" asked Maddie, "I got another modeling gig."

"How many is that now?" asked Vivian.

"Four. The academy, the university, a community college and a private studio." She paused. "I think I found the guy I'm going to marry. But he doesn't know it, yet!"

"One of the art students?"

"No. The janitor at the academy!"

Thomas appeared with an armful of chairs he had carried from the house. Darla closed the door behind him and took one of the chairs.

"It's looking good in here," Thomas said.

Velma had moved all the woodworking machines to the side, thrown a rug next to the stove and created an intimate seating area for her guests. On a low crate, there was a dish of candied nuts and dried figs.

Maddie was the first to reach a score of one-hundred and celebrated her victory with a saucy dance around the bucket of firewood. Hannah flipped over the tablet filled with Maddie's not-always-truthful figures and wrote a short message. Thomas returned to the house to collect more supplies as Darla resumed her work on the decorations.

Hannah made her way across the shop to stand beside Darla and slipped her the note.

Frank asked me to marry him.

"Congratulations," Darla signed. "It isn't a surprise. How long have you been dating him?"

"Four years." She shrugged her shoulders as if to admit the proposal was a long time coming.

Vivian and Maddie spread a large, single cloth over the table.

There was a knock on the door. It would be Thomas with a stackful of plates. But when Vivian opened it, Naomi and Larry stepped inside.

"Hello, everybody," Naomi said. "Merry Christmas!" She was holding a perfectly prepared fruitcake, crowned with a ring of maraschino cherries and toasted pecans.

"You made this yourself?" Maddie asked, taking the confection, laying claim to it.

"I did. But we can't overlook Larry. I might be Mrs. Claus but we rode in on Larry's sleigh." She laughed just a bit too loudly at her eye-rolling metaphor.

Everyone could see they were having an affair, but Hannah forgave Naomi's giddiness, knowing nowhere else could Naomi feel so unrestrained and reveal her affections so openly. The couple had been secretly seeing one other, off and on, for nearly six years.

"You're welcome to stay for dinner," Vivian said. "We won't be eating for another few hours."

"We have to run along," Naomi said, "before I'm missed." She laughed nervously and blew Hannah a kiss. "After the new year, we'll have another tête-à-tête."

Admiring the tree, Hannah noticed behind it a rocking chair on the work counter. She approached it cautiously.

"Oh, my goodness!" she exclaimed.

"What?" asked Vivian.

"The rocking chair. It was mine. It once belonged to me."

"What's it doing here?" asked Maddie.

"It was sold at the auction. Look. Here's the mark when Simon lost a front tooth."

Vivian joined Hannah. "It was brought in to be refinished. I don't know by whom. Velma can tell you more."

Hannah imagined the mark would be sanded away and the chair covered with a coat of fresh paint. How old was Simon when he tripped over the rug and fell against the rocking chair? Six? He would be nineteen now. Gerald would be twenty-one. They could have been good friends with Thomas.

Velma and Thomas entered the shop with plates and a silverware chest.

"Have you seen the napkins?" Velma asked Vivian.

Darla held up a handful of pressed napkins and gestured, "Is this what you're looking for?"

After setting down the dishes, Velma threw a log into the stove.

A car was heard driving up.

"Who could that be?" Vivian wondered aloud.

"It's probably Dewey," Velma said. "Here to pick up his wife's Christmas gift."

"Dewey?! Maddie said, nearly choking.

"Do you know him?" inquired Velma.

A knock was heard on the door. Maddie jumped up, looking for a place where she might hide. It had been ten years since Maddie, under layers of thick paint, accosted Mad Dewey, but she was fearful nonetheless. Perhaps Dewey would recognize her breath or the curve and bulk of her broad shoulders.

"Dewey," Velma said, opening the door. "I was expecting you."

Dewey removed his hat and surveyed the room. "Hello, Hannah."

"Dewey."

Velma explained. "Dewey had me repair an old medicine cabinet that belonged to his wife's parents."

Dewey parked himself by the stove, grateful for the heat, rubbing his hands together. He peered at Maddie. "You look familiar. Do I know you?"

"I don't believe so."

"What's your name?"

A wide-eyed Maddie stammered, "Judith Soloway. Professional stenographer!"

"Are you from around here?"

Hannah stepped forward. "Judith, I believe it's time to go put the pies in the oven."

"Pies?" questioned Dewey.

"Apple."

"I hope they're from my orchard!"

Maddie began inching toward the door.

"With a handful of walnuts and raisins. And served, I expect, with excellent vanilla ice cream."

Maddie eased the door open and quickly slipped out.

"I hope your wife likes her gift," Velma said encouragingly.

After Dewey left, Hannah questioned Velma, "Has Dewey changed?"

"I don't know. What do you mean? How so?"

"He used to always smell of liquor," Hannah said.

*****

*****

Frank was taking a shower as Hannah sat on the edge of the bed and looked around the room. "Could I live here?" she asked herself. "Could I make this my home?" Slowly, she got up and made her way about the room, testing it for an answer she already knew. She caught the faintest trace of soap scent, which made her smile. She paused by the dresser and gazed at the sketches of Frank and Norma, then picked up the pile of papers next to them. They were a series of drawings by Darla, scenes from the Paulson farm, done years ago. Hannah returned to the bed and sat down to linger over the drawings. Little scenes of farm life. Several bales of straw waiting to be unloaded. A discarded tractor tire. The latch of a barn door not fully engaged. A metal container for holding fuel on a work bench.

She stopped, breathless, staring at the sketch. With a rising sense of fear, she reached over to retrieve her reading glasses from the nightstand, to examine the drawing more closely.

The shower was turned off.

Devastated, confused, Hannah stared at the picture. In it was a drawing of the gasoline can left behind at LeRoy's farm. The match was unmistakable. In both cases the word in large block lettering painted on the can – *KEROCENE* – misspelled.

A small cry escaped her. She jumped up and replaced the drawings. She stared at the framed drawing of Frank, not comprehending what she saw, frozen. Slowly she made her way back to the bed, sat down and put on her shoes.

Frank entered the bedroom. Instantly he realized something in Hannah had changed. "What's wrong?"

"I can't continue this," Hannah said.

"What?" Frank said in disbelief.

"We can't go on."

"What are you saying? What's come over you?"

Hannah stood up. "I have to go."

"Would you tell me what's going on!" pleaded Frank.

"I can't talk to you right now...."

"Please! I have a right to know!"

She looked at him with disbelief. "Frank, oh dear, Frank, I'm so sorry...." She turned, walked out the door and ran down the stairs, tears streaming down her face.

*****

*****

Goodbye Michelle, it's hard to die
When all the birds are singing in the sky
Now that spring is in the air
With flowers everywhere
I wish that we could both be there.

"Terry Jacks," the announcer said. "*Seasons in the Sun* inspired by the French song writer, Jacques Brel."

Hannah turned off the radio and turned to Thomas. "That's enough sad for today."

They were driving to St. Louis to attend Darla's graduation. After the ceremony, they would pack up all her supplies, spend the night with Wanda and Derek and head back the next day.

"How is house hunting?" Hannah asked Thomas.

"Nothing seems right so far."

"Oh?"

"I'd like a place with a sun room or, maybe, an enclosed porch."

"Couldn't you build a studio? A little space with lots of windows?"

"I could, I suppose."

"Larry would help you."

"And there's always Velma. She's handy, too."

"And your wedding plans?"

"Thankfully Darla's in charge of that. She wants to keep it small."

"Be sure to invite Sheriff Wilson."

Several miles passed in silence.

"Can I ask you something personal?" asked Thomas.

"Anything. You may not like the answer."

Thomas paused, took a breath, then said, "How did your family die?"

Hannah turned on the windshield wiper and pushed the washer button to clear it of bugs.

"I'm sorry. You don't need to say. It's really none of my business," Thomas said.

"My husband and both my boys were found inside the silo, overcome by nitrogen dioxide. How did it happen? I don't know. I wasn't there."

*****

Had Hannah been able to witness the scene, she would have known this truth:

After blowing the day's harvest into the silo, Horace knew the container was about to reach its capacity. The boys were curious. Gerald climbed the outside cage ladder. Simon went into the barn and climbed the cover chute, with its series of wooden, removable unloading doors. On his climb, while reaching for an overhead rung, Simon scratched a door panel, catching a splinter under his fingernail. When he reached the top, Gerald was already there, standing on the filling platform, opposite him. Another eight feet of fodder and the silo would be full.

"Throw me your pocket knife," Simon requested. "I have a splinter."

Gerald fumbled for the knife in his pocket. He threw it across the silo to Simon.

He failed to catch the pocketknife; it fell into the silo.

Before Gerald could yell, "No," Simon had jumped into the silo and begun searching for the pocketknife. The more he fumbled around to seize the knife, the deeper it fell into the fodder. He began coughing violently, staggered for a moment, then collapsed.

"Dad!" Gerald yelled. "Simon needs help!" From the opposite side he jumped, intending to rescue his brother.

Horace came running and scampered up the outside ladder.

When he reached the top and saw Gerald gasping for air, struggling to revive Simon, he knew he had to climb back down and climb up the covered chute and remove a series of unloading doors to free his sons.

When Horace reached the top of the chute ladder, he saw both sons had been overcome with fumes. He removed two doors and threw them down the chute. The third was stuck. No amount of prying could loosen it. Horace climbed over the stuck door and jumped into the silo. Somehow, he would have to lift his sons six feet and drape them over the top door, without letting them fall down the chute. Or, perhaps he could claw his way up, even though there were no handholds to assist him … .

Of course, the truth was forever hidden, never to be revealed.

Hannah only knew her husband and two sons were dead. Overcome by fumes, they had suffocated to death. Over the years she would construct a thousand scenarios as to what happened that day. None gave her peace. None exorcised the demons.

*****

*****

"I don't see the sense of it," Frances declared. "A mother not allowed to be with her daughter at the birth of her first grandchild."

"What about me?" Thomas said. "I'm her husband."

"Well, that's different," Frances replied. "As any woman who gave birth can tell you, we understand these things."

Quincy gave Thomas a sorry-I-can't-help-you look.

Frances continued. "And another thing. I don't understand this trend of at-home births." She glared at Thomas as if he were solely responsible for the decision. "Where did this idea come from?" she asked, glancing at Hannah. "Art school?"

Hannah and Thomas exchanged looks. Three years had passed since Darla graduated from Washburn Art Academy, to which Frances attributed any unbecoming behavior on the part of her daughter.

Frances was not done. "A midwife is not a doctor!" she concluded.

"This could go on for hours," Hannah said. "We need to pass the time somehow. Thomas, pull the GMC around. We'll wax my truck."

Thomas parked the van near the house, a narrow two-story Victorian structure with two gables and a side porch, enclosed with windows.

"Thomas, is there a ladder in the shed we can use?"

When Thomas returned with the ladder he first placed it against the sill of the bedroom window. Cautiously he climbed the rungs to peer inside, hoping to catch a glimpse of the happenings. In no time, the midwife raised the window and shooed Thomas away. Leaning out the opening she kept a watchful eye on Thomas until he removed the ladder. She closed the shutters.

"Darla painted this sign," Hannah explained as she polished the side of the truck. "That was before she went to art school. And look at her now, with her own studio and about to become a mother."

They heard a muffled scream coming from the bedroom.

"A midwife is no doctor," Frances repeated.

"Thomas, be prepared. Darla will be spending a lot of time making portraits of your child," Hannah predicted.

Thomas appeared not to have heard. He was listening for any sound that might indicate their child had arrived. Having finished buffing the roof of the van, he climbed down the ladder.

Once again he positioned the ladder, leaning it against the shutters, and started to climb. He was nearly at the top, hoping to peer between the slats, when the midwife threw open the shutters and announced, "It's a girl!"

Thomas landed on the ground on his back with a deadening thud.

*****

*****

Having promised weeks in advance to be there, Hannah pulled into the driveway of the woodworking shop, next to Velma and Vivian's home. Darla was the first to greet her, running from the porch to throw her arms around Hannah. So ebullient was her spirit, Hannah wondered if she were pregnant again. Molly, two years old, wasn't far behind, running so fast her little legs barely held her up. Hannah gathered Molly up in her arms and greeted her with a long, sweet kiss.

They made their way up the walk, toward the house where Thomas was waiting in his wheelchair. Hannah gave his hand a squeeze.

Vivian, with Velma's help, backed out of the house, carrying an overstuffed chair.

"What's going on?" Hannah asked.

"A concert," Vivian replied. They carried the chair down the porch steps and placed it on the grass. "A concert on the lawn.

"Please take a seat," Velma told Hannah.

The couple tilted back Thomas in his wheelchair and eased it down the steps. Darla unfurled several blankets that were draped over the porch railing.

A concert?" Hannah said. "Who's performing?"

Thomas pointed to the roof of the shop. On the chimney, Velma had attached a large flared speaker.

"I haven't any idea," Thomas said sheepishly, as Velma set out a picnic basket, jug of lemonade and party noisemakers.

"Naomi couldn't be here, but she sent a container of her homemade banana ice cream," Velma announced.

Nathan came out of the shop, carrying a large radio. He was joined by Velma who uncoiled an electric cord as Darla unraveled the speaker wire.

"This is a lot of fuss for a concert," Hannah observed.

"Oh, the concert isn't just for us. It's for all of Kalb County." Nathan, who'd been keeping close track of the time, turned on the radio. It was the top of the hour and the start of the *Kenny Pratt Show*.

The voice of the announcer flooded the homestead and surrounding area.

After broadcasting the usual pleasantries, Kenny was ready to launch into his program. "Making his debut tonight," Kenny announced, "Is LeRoy Williams, one-time resident of Kalb County, with his song *More Than You and Me*. Here's LeRoy!"

> We have a place, you and me
> There's a garden that needs tending
> There's a fence that needs mending

Hannah felt someone wrap his arms around her from behind. She turned to see LeRoy. "Oh, my goodness," she cried, grabbing both his wrists. "LeRoy! That's you!" She pointed to the speakers. Ethel and Sam joined them.

> We share a child, you and me
> There's a son who needs providing
> There's a dad in need of guiding

There was a bridge between the stanzas, filled with LeRoy riffing on the guitar. "How we've missed you," Hannah told Ethel. "You must be so proud!"

> Let's right a wrong, you and me
> There's a war that needs an ending
> There's a cause that needs defending.
>
> We seek a song, you and me
> There's a tune that needs playing
> There's a story in need of saying.
>
> We hold a million dreams, you and me
> But living their reality
> Takes more than you and me

*****

*****

It was three-o-seven on Saturday, August 14, 1982 when the call came. Hannah was cleaning the bathroom in her small, rented cottage. It took a moment to maneuver herself out of the cramped quarters.

"Hello."

"Eli knows."

"Naomi?"

"Eli found out about Larry and me." Naomi sounded desperate.

"How did he find out?"

"I don't know. Hannah, I'm scared."

"How can I help?"

"Eli is on his way to confront Larry. I tried calling Larry, to warn him, but he doesn't answer. What am I going to do?"

"Have you called the police."

"No. Should I?"

"I think that would be a good idea. Ask them to go to Willow Tree Apartments."

"When Eli returns, I'm afraid he's going to hurt me."

"Where are you now?" Hannah asked.

"I couldn't stay at home. I drove over to the church." Her voice was quivering, "Hannah, I really love Larry. Something terrible is going to happen. I just know it."

"Stay there," Hannah said. "I'm coming over."

Naomi broke down. "Would you?" She hung up.

Hannah washed her hands, gathered up her keys and ran to the van. She spun the truck around, kicking up stones – something Nathan would not fail to notice – and headed toward Creekside Mennonite Church.

She expected Naomi to be waiting for her by the front door. She was not. As Hannah made her way toward the sanctuary she sensed it was uncomfortably quiet.

"Naomi?" she called, pushing open the door.

She walked through the foyer, into the sanctuary. There, hanging from the rafters was Naomi, lifeless. Under her was a step ladder, lying on its side.

Hannah approached her friend, tears beginning to stream down her cheeks. "No, Naomi. No." She looked up, into her face, "It didn't need to end this way."

She noticed an envelope tucked under Naomi's belt. Only the "h's" were visible, but Hannah knew it was meant for her. She up-righted the step ladder and climbed several steps to retrieve the envelope, then laid the ladder back down.

The note was brief.

> Hannah, Thank you for everything.
> I never got my black rose.

Hannah turned the notecard over.

> Tell Larry I'm sorry and that I love him.
> I was wrong. Larry was my black rose.

*****

*****

Eli was accompanied by several police officers.

"How did you know Naomi was here?"

"She called me," Hannah said.

"Do you have any idea why she'd take her life?" Officer Harden asked.

"Yes."

"Can you tell us?"

"That's a question for Eli," Hannah said.

"There could have been many reasons," Eli said. "Naomi wasn't a well person."

Hannah took hold of the back of a pew, feeling her anger rise.

Eli turned to her. "Did she leave a note?"

Hannah remained silent

"I'll take that as a yes," Eli said. "Don't you take that as a yes, Officer?"

"Yes." Hannah replied. "She left a note."

"I'd like to see it."

"It had my name on the envelope."

"I have a right to see it."

"It's confidential."

"I think, by law, I have a right to see it."

"This isn't a crime scene," Hannah answered. "This is a suicide."

Mr. Harden interrupted. "Perhaps we can take this up later. I'd like to have the body removed as soon as the coroner gives his consent."

Eli sat on the front pew.

From where she stood, Hannah said slowly, "I know the church has strict rules. I hope you'll overlook them and allow your wife to be buried here."

The point did not go unnoticed. Victims of suicide were not considered members in good standing, having severed their obedience to the will of God.

"If I'm no longer needed here," Hannah said to Officer Harden, "I would like to leave."

*****

*****

Perhaps not the most renowned gallery in St. Louis, *The Loge* was a close second. Clarence Sutton, who taught at Washburn Art Academy, was an advisor to *The Loge*'s director. Almost once a year Clarence visited Darla to check on her progress, to learn what new ideas had captured her interest. It was he who orchestrated the one-woman show.

Nathan had borrowed a passenger van to accommodate the group. Slipping his hands under Thomas' armpits, Nathan clumsily hoisted him into the front passenger seat. Velma stowed the collapsed wheelchair next to the spare tire. She and Vivian took the back seat and motioned for Darla to hand off the box with Darla's dress, the one she would change into that evening. Hannah and Darla settled in the middle seat, designed for two, but six-year-old Molly snuggled in between them.

"You'll have more room back here, Molly," Vivian said.

Molly ignored the invitation to move.

"Are we ready?" asked Nathan, his hand on the gear shift.

Thomas turned to face his wife. "Are you excited?" he signed.

Darla nodded, "Yes."

The show had been hung early in the week. They were going to the galley where Darla could preview the work, then out for a late lunch, returning to the gallery later for the reception. They would be joined by Wanda and Maddie.

"Molly," requested Vivian, "ask your mother if her parents are coming to see the show."

Molly translated the question to Darla who answered in sign.

"They're leaving later this afternoon," Molly announced, brushing back her hair.

Hannah smiled at the gesture. Molly, who sometimes accompanied Hannah on her rounds, frequently reminded her of her mother.

"Who are you interviewing this week?" Thomas asked Nathan.

"A pair of twins who are raising a pair of sheep, two pigs and a couple of chickens. Part of a *4-H* project. Or maybe it's *FFA*. I'm not sure."

"What's *FFA*?" asked Molly.

"*Future Farmers of America.*"

"Can I join?"

"You want to get into the raising-barnyard-animals business?"

"Who knows, Papa? Your daughter may become a vetnarian."

"Veterinarian," corrected Nathan. "V. E. T. E. R. I. N. A. R. I. A. N."

"And the winner of the adult division spelling bee is Nathan Proctor. As always," quipped Velma.

"Tell Thomas," urged Vivian.

"Oh, yes. Thomas. Those veneers of Zebrawood finally arrived."

"Were they worth the price?"

"I think so. But it's your money, not mine."

When Molly was three, Thomas had asked Velma if he could make a dollhouse for Molly in her woodshop. It was a handsome endeavor, earning enthusiastic compliments from the couple's friends. Thomas began a second dollhouse and with Velma's guidance his crafting skills quickly improved. Now he worked two days a week in the shop, building up a growing business for his Victorian creations. The remaining three days of the week Thomas worked as a cashier at Darlington's Grocery Store.

Darla's show was entitled *Kaleidoscope: Kalb County*. It was a series of eighteen collages, each three feet by four feet. For each piece, Darla had selected a black and white photograph of a farm in Kalb County. Each photo was duplicated seven times. The original became the master photo. The remaining six photos each received a toning bath. One was saturated with yellow, the others tinted in hues of blue, green, violet, brown and red. Darla then choose a quilt pattern; its geometric shapes were imposed over various parts of the master image. The design template was duplicated on each of the six colored photographs. Darla cut and removed hundreds of small squares, triangles and rectangles from the master, replacing them with their colored counterparts. Rather than gluing the reassembled designs in place, they were stitched together. Parts of the master photograph were untouched. Some shapes were discarded and never replaced, leaving the space empty.

Darla was greeted by Clarence and the gallery director, Tad Mosel. The group dispersed to view the collages, while the evening's schedule was explained through signs and notes to Darla.

The Williams Farm, twice sold since LeRoy moved his family to Detroit, incorporated two similar quilt designs: the *Missouri Star* and the *Broken Star*. Their placement, like two opposing forces navigating the landscape, created a dynamic sense of visual conflict.

The rows of fruit trees on Dewey's Orchard were accented with a *Flying Geese* pattern. The details of the packing shed and outbuildings disappeared under the deep contrasting triangles of *Return of the Swallows*.

The fields of the Leichty farmstead had been married, somewhat sentimentally, to a *Garden of Eden* design.

Most of the farms were recognizable. The old Mercer farm, sunlit and deeply shadowed. The Paulson farm on a rainy day. The designs stitched into the photographs, *Pinwheels, Corn and Beans, Old Maid's Puzzle, Combination Star*, were familiar, found on quilts hanging on Kalb County wash lines or adorning beds.

At the entrance to the gallery there was a didactic, describing Darla and her work. Next to it was a small frame, unlike any of the other works in the gallery. It held Darla's first sketch of Hannah's Metro, done twenty-one years ago, which Hannah had kept in the secret compartment of her vans. Behind the drawing was a single quilt patch.

The title card read: "All the quilt designs in this exhibition are traditional patterns. This, however, is an original design which I call *Hannah's Star*."

*****

*****

Three Eyes was curled up in Molly's lap as Hannah pulled into the gas station.

"I'm feeling a little warm," Hannah said. "Would you mind getting me a coke, Molly?"

Molly searched through Hannah's purse for loose change.

"I think when I finish this season, I'm going to retire."

In the last few years, Hannah had reduced the number of routes from eight to five. She was sixty-four and beginning to feel her age.

"Does that mean you'll come live with us?" asked Molly.

"We'll see. Your mother can be very persistent." She made the sign for strong-willed. "Get yourself a drink, too."

Tucking Three Eyes under her arm, Molly stepped out of the truck and crossed to the outdoor vending machine.

When the mechanic winked at her, she rolled her eyes and snapped, "Don't you know better than to make a pass at a twelve-year-old girl!"

She returned to the driver's side and was about to hand the coke through the window, when she noticed Hannah slumped over, her head forward, her arms wrapped around the steering wheel.

Molly screamed and the mechanic came running.

*****

*****

The mechanic refused to drive the truck. Instead, he towed it to Thomas and Darla's home. That evening Velma and Vivian joined the family.

"I built a secret compartment in a cabinet in the truck," Velma said, "similar to the one in Hannah's first van. I think we should open it and see if there is anything that might be useful to know."

The boxes from the hidden drawer were placed on the kitchen table where Darla, Velma and Vivian began to sort through the papers and keepsakes.

From among the items, the women selected several documents and sealed them in an envelope.

At the gravesite, Molly stepped forward. Fearless, she lifted Hannah's shroud and slipped the envelope under it.

The envelope contained a forged burial certificate from the Director of Zoning at Kalb County Courthouse allowing for the home burial of Horace, Gerald, and Simon Mercer, a false document stating that Judith Soloway was a certified stenographer, and a fabricated license to do business under the name, *Hannah's Goods & Effects*.